The Sonnets

The Sonnets

Warwick Collins

The Friday Project
An imprint of HarperCollins Publishers
77–85 Fulham Palace Road
Hammersmith, London W6 8JB
www.thefridayproject.co.uk
www.harpercollins.co.uk

First published by The Friday Project in 2008
This paperback edition published by The Friday Project in 2009

A catalogue record for this book is available
from the British Library

ISBN 978-0-00-730619-0

Typeset by Maggie Dana
Printed and bound in Great Britain by Clays Ltd, St Ives plc

Mixed Sources

Product group from well-managed
forests and other controlled sources
www.fsc.org   Cert no. SW-COC-1806
© 1996 Forest Stewardship Council

FSC

FSC is a non-profit international organisation established to
promote the responsible management of the world's forests. Products
carrying the FSC label are independently certified to assure
consumers that they come from forests that are managed to meet the
social, economic and ecological needs of present or future
generations.

Find out more about HarperCollins and the environment at
www.harpercollins.co.uk/green

To Chris Owen

Chapter 1

MY LORD SOUTHAMPTON, at the lake that day, removed his garments, wading in silence to deeper water. In hungry dawn his slender frame, already bearing scars and calluses of fearful games and hunts, seemed to pause and flicker. A heron stood on the neighbouring bank, observing the edge of the shallows. Against that human figure a bird's shadow, hovering over water, preparing to strike at waiting fish, would not have seemed more ghostly or more pale. There my lord waited, hardly moving, suspended in the heron's eye, as though lost in invisible thought.

I, standing on the shore, observed how light became flesh, seeming to pause and thicken. Water covered his thighs, his lower back. From the bank I considered him as he walked further into the lake, until it lapped his shoulder blades. I continued to observe him as he waded deeper into that periphrastic calm. The liquid line rose until, once level with shoulder and neck, he began to swim, both languidly and strongly.

Out there he seemed impalpable. Only his head appeared, floating on the surface. Under the dawn light he moved alongside his own reflection, touching ghost to liquid ghost, leaving a soft wake which formed and glimmered like an arrowhead.

Instead it was I – the watching man, the unquiet one – who took up my usual position, holding the reins of both our nervous horses. Part of that mind which lives in shadow now became alert. I remained constantly fretful – the silent waiter at the water's edge.

Standing between the horses in that calm, with a warm and breathing beast on each side of me, I sensed the shudder of their animal spirits. Both seemed tense. My own gelding stood still, occasionally reaching down to feed. But beside me the stallion stamped and neighed softly, dancing on his hooves, restless as any child who wants to play. He was in perpetual motion, never still. I felt him strain, then call forth his challenge. His long whinny reached out across the tranquil earth and water. Holding their reins, I listened for that thread of silence which the horses could perceive. And then I heard, as though in answer, another horse's call, as clear as a bugle note, from half a mile away; from some dark stretch of woodland, some invisible valley. Strange sound! It might as easily have come from a mythical, hidden underworld.

During those times when the London theatres were closed, curtailed by plague, I too was nervous, aware of my own vulnerability. My scribbling of plays had no market, and I could not even work upon the stage. It is true that poets often live at the edge of starvation – vulnerable as song birds to winter's cold – but those days were the worst.

By some strange alchemy, my lord's very confidence rendered me more sensitive. On his behalf sometimes I felt we were overlooked, or that another party spied on him. Sometimes I heard a horse neigh, far away, and once I saw three riders on a hill – distant, pricked out by light – observing us in what seemed like lucid concentration.

He began to swim now into the deeper part of the lake, so that the shadow of his body dissolved in the water. Only his head appeared, like a bust, floating on the milky surface. I stood a little back from the bank's edge, ever-watchful.

Though he was my patron, I continued to chafe at his recklessness. For these were dangerous times, with many eddies of insurrection around our Protestant Queen. His family retained their allegiance to the Catholic Church. In their midst, he moved with peculiar ease, and feared nothing.

Out on the water, my lord turned, treading water, and looked back towards the silent land. Could he perceive me, soberly coloured against the darker earth? Even at that distance, I could see there was amusement in his expression. He called out, 'Will you not swim, Master Shakespeare?'

I did not answer.

'Come, gentle man,' he sang out. 'Swim with me.'

I, the nominative, smiled to myself and answered, 'I prefer to keep a watch, my lord!'

'Come,' he repeated. 'The animals will not run far. If they do, we'll catch 'em.'

Alas, he thought my concern was with the horses. Around us lay an unsettled land. The woods had spies in them, and there were those whose loyalty was to the other great families – a number of whom did not wish him well. Yet he regarded himself as invulnerable. If I were not here, he would have let the horses wander and have happily chased them for a morning, naked and alone, without a thought for himself or for those who might see him in a state of nature.

Out on the lake my lord still swam. Now he turned and sang out to me in his clear, melodious voice, 'Come, live with me, and be my love, and we will all the pleasures prove.'

I observed him laugh at his own joke – knowing that he quoted Christopher Marlowe at me, and aware that it fretted at my profession of poet and incited my jealousy. He enjoyed reminding me that our great Marlowe also vied for his patronage. Perhaps, too, he relished the suggestion that Marlowe would be more responsive than I to his playful overtures. And since my patron, though young, was a man of subtlety and mischief, his remark reminded me that Master Marlowe was invited to dine at his house that night, during which time, no doubt, we two poets would be teased like rival and delicate young mistresses.

Perhaps my lord realised that I would not abandon my lookout. He shook his head at my caution, smiled to himself, turned, and swam out further into the lake.

Chapter 2

STRANGE TO OBSERVE, yet stranger to recall, were those who called my lord ladylike, affected, languorous. Around him I observed his acolytes gather and whisper. Yet all who bore close witness to his pale beauty also observed, beneath the liquid surface, the stir of muscle and sinew. A condign will fleshed the hidden currents of the water. The searching eye, bent towards its surface, recognised fierce pride, and cold reflection. It was true that he was one of those who are unaware of how he scattered light. The effect was that all those admiring glances, falling on that surface, were reflected backwards to their source. In that way, he was like all heroes: you saw what you hoped for; he refracted your dreams.

Unaware of his own power, such grace seemed strange to him as much as to his companions. Yet to write of him as Narcissus, in truth, was also to address another. Rumours moved around him. He was there and not there, laughing at those vanities attributed to him by others. During the plague years, when the London theatres were closed, I saw my own fond hopes and circling ambitions reflected in that youthful, mirthful glass. He was both my plight and my aspiration.

As for effeminacy, in those surroundings what argument could one propose for such a creature? There were other realms, even in our own society, where effeminacy was much admired. In our theatre companies women were forbidden to act on the stage; beautiful boys and young men played the female roles, and were celebrated for their virtuosity. I myself loved their ambivalence; the flavour of the unknown and forbidden beneath the formal inhibition. Maleness might be enforced in the theatre, but not masculinity.

Our martial aristocracy, by contrast, lived by bloodlines. Twenty generations of great Pharaohs might create inbred leaders with perfect skin and lissom hips, but our turbulent kingdom, always on the edge of war, gave cruel tests to its warriors, often allowing less than a man's brief span before disease or death, the axe-man, struck them down. Their deepest truths were brutal, simply this: all their lives hovered on the verge of annihilation. And these, our politic-ridden times, allowed no easy settlement into placidity or plain repose.

If we were sometimes witness to things of grace, it was by contrast rather than by inherence. Stare into fire, see how the greatest heat lies like a mellow ghost on wood or coal. So, in the harshness of our age, such a youth, whose fair exterior floated as a fervent dream before our eyes, was at the limit of benign possibility.

But grace itself is a form of power, carrying its own hidden and implicit threat. If I myself survived and even thrived in my lord's companionship, it was precisely because, beneath that surface, I never forgot the harsh heat of his potency. I attempted to describe something of his character in a sonnet I was writing, addressing as its subject the nature of his attractions to those in his circle, his reflection of their dreams:

What is your substance, whereof are you made,
That millions of strange shadows on you tend?
Since every one hath, every one, one shade,
And you, but one, can every shadow lend.
Describe Adonis, and the counterfeit
Is poorly imitated after you;
On Helen's cheek all art of beauty set,
And you in Grecian tires are painted new:
Speak of the spring and foison of the year,
The one doth shadow of your beauty show,
The other as your bounty doth appear;
And you in every blessed shape we know.
*   In all external grace you have some part,*
*   But you like none, none you, for constant heart.*

That 'constant heart' I attributed to him was not a mere conceit, or a pretty figure of speech. He was my patron, my source of life in those bad times, and every waking day I thanked my good fortune for his loyalty.

As for myself, my own beginnings had been strange. When, after several years as a travelling player, I began to try out a line or two, to help my fellow actors with a scene – bridging an awkward pause here, helping to refine a phrase there – it seemed to me no more than journeyman's work. But then, like an artisan found amongst gentlefolk, my own poor skills became more valuable. 'This ending appears too long, would you say?', or 'Could we not fit an extra scene here?' Silver-tongued, I mouthed the words, worrying back and forth upon the stage, adjusting entrances, reworking rhythms, waving my arms in emphasis, bowing, stooping to kiss imagined ladies' hands, learning meanwhile the practical difference between iambic *di dah* or trochaic *dah di,* or how to use the two long beats of a spondee to add occasional emphasis.

Here I stand, a mere grammar-school boy, risen wit, obsequious survivor, forced to rely for my living on the ancient tradition of a line of warriors. Should I plead for aristocracy or heritance? No, let the dice fall where they may. Yet here were no effete men, but soldiers, soldiers' sons, robbers, intimidators. Above the ranks of *villeins* rose the lords, greater villains all, whose hidden power lay not in virtue or principle, but the hissing edge of axe or broadsword or skull-crushing mace. In France they say *chevalier,* meaning horseman, from whose high mount, delivering painful punishment or death, a little mercy sometimes followed. Hence the code of chivalric virtue.

These were the men I lived among, who asked and gave no quarter to themselves; jealous of bloodlines, but hardly bloodless, fierce in pride, quick to anger, remorseless in revenge. In my lord's household those were the local spirits who inhabited his terrain.

Chapter 3

I REMEMBER, as though it were yesterday, my horse's heavy breathing as it strained its heaving chest against the night air. The large house loomed close. My sturdy mount cantered, jingling bridle and reins, until the stonework reared out of the darkness, with braziers burning at its entrance.

I rode through the main gate, past gargoyles and heraldic stone roses, into walled gardens. My lord's house at Titchfield had once been an abbey, confiscated from the monks by our monarch's father, granted as gift to my lord's grandfather – the first Earl of

Southampton – by Henry VIII. The buildings still retained their atmosphere of contemplation.

In the courtyard I dismounted. A stable boy, emerging from the dark, took my horse and led it away.

In my best clothes – a doublet and hose, with a rakish hat and a tattered black cloak – I stepped forward, striding towards a doorway from which there came the noise of men laughing. Passing through, I faced on my left side a great dining hall, with a long table at which were seated thirty or so guests and retainers of the house. I looked towards the head of the table where my lord presided, and bowed my head to his presence.

On his right there was an empty place. On his left sat a singular, dark, saturnine man, whose intelligent eyes surveyed me.

'Master Shakespeare!' my lord called out. Holding my attention, he indicated the vacant seat near him with a finger's tap, so that I went to my allotted place, sliding my legs under the table. 'You have not met Master Marlowe before?'

'In passing,' I replied.

Beside my patron the figure stirred its languid length, as if his wit steeled itself.

'Then in that passing,' Marlowe said, 'we did not meet.'

Though casual, all conversation on the great table seemed to cease.

Around me the silence seemed somehow both decisive and complete. My lord, too, considered me. I felt as though a French fencing master, contemptuously and elegantly, had flicked a fly off my cloak with the point of his sword, as though to say, 'I may choose to strike when I will.' The whole hall watched me suffer their regard. For several moments it seemed as though I were about to fall.

But I am an actor, and I know that timing is all. The performer inside me rose to the occasion, sensing the drama, even milking the moment for its worth. That same congregation noted my own answering stillness, observed me incline my head in calm acknowledgement of my rival's superior artistry. So it seemed from the first fateful meeting that we two poets were doomed to consider each other – from our different perspectives – like rivals about to engage.

'Tell me, Master Shakespeare,' my lord asked, allowing himself to throw casual extra fuel on our vanities, and playing to the gallery. 'Tell me now, according to their virtue, which of Master Marlowe's plays do you prefer?'

His directness made me smile, despite my fear. His pure thirst for entertainment was as clear as a hunter's horn on a still day. Noting at the same time how the rest of the company continued their watchfulness, hoping for sport, I too became temporarily silent, as though hunting with them.

'You are considering, are you, Master Shakespeare?' my patron said.

'My lord,' I replied, 'from all I have read of Master Marlowe, there is too much richness to easily contemplate.'

I remember the nature and depth of that silence. From its centre a small ripple of applause moved outwards at this diplomatic answer, spreading round the table. Even Master Marlowe smiled. My lord, too, seemed pleased at the *frisson*. But he persisted. 'And now that you have had time to consider your answer, what think you?'

'I believe,' I began, 'that I admire most, before *The Jew of Malta*, even before *Doctor Faustus* ... *Hero and Leander*.'

There was another silence. A small, clear frown formed on my lord's forehead. 'Come now, is this a riddle? Who here has heard of *Hero and Leander?*'

Our host turned towards the other poet. 'I believe he teases you, Master Marlowe. By citing a play that does not exist, he surely incites your retribution.'

Cold and calm, the one he addressed spoke out. 'No, my lord, what he says is true. Except this: the work in question is not a play but a poem. And it exists, as yet unfinished.'

The rival poet turned towards me, detached enquiry in those fierce, dark eyes. He asked, with a deceptive limpidity, 'And how is it, Master Shakespeare, that you have read my own unfinished work?'

But by then I had begun to gauge the feelings of that waiting audience; its liking for directness, its hunger for incisive clarities. I said, 'You are so famed, sir, that copies of it circulate.' I gestured with my hand in visible circles, so that one or two of the watchers laughed.

His next words were carefully chosen, laid out like chess pieces on a board. 'And you make it your business to read it?'

The question's coldness touched me somewhere deep. But if I am a player, I am used to contingency, to turn and pivot. So I responded, hearing myself say, 'What I most admire, I fear. And what I most fear, I admire.'

As if by instinct – though not greater skill – I had cause to believe his sword was turned; or that, passing through me, his blade found no flesh, no bone to hasp. From the long table I heard again that limpid, expectant silence, and then a rising ripple of applause.

My lord seemed pleased at this exchange. He had played on our rivalry, enjoyed his sport. His restless mind moved to other subjects. And so, to my own relief, he began to discourse with others, while the applause died down and the table settled again to its eating and interrupted conversations.

A little later, my lord touched me on the shoulder in support, signalling that constant affection for which he was both praised and slandered, whispering in my ear, 'Well spoken, sir,' while from the other side of that long table Master Marlowe looked on, saturnine and amused, keeping his thoughts to himself.

The dinner reached its end, the candles flickered.

Some of the guests lay forward on the table, drunk. My lord surveyed the scene with approval, saying, 'It seems that we are surfeited.'

I, by nature more cautious and abstemious than the others, nodded to where Marlowe also lay forward, asleep on his arms. Of the visiting poet my lord said softly, 'Let us not wake him. He rode from London, where it is said he conspires constantly with the younger Walsingham. Let him sleep.'

He turned towards me. 'Come, now, let us play a game of throw-apple, and while we may, wake certain of these diners.'

He plucked an apple from a dish of fruit in front of him, and rose from his seat. Gathering my wits, I followed him as he walked alongside the great table, shaking awake various of his guests. A number rose and stumbled after him, mumbling to themselves as though in a dream. I took hold of one of the torches that lay against the wall, lit it from the last of the burning logs, and followed the young earl out into the cold air of the courtyard.

The drunken company followed behind. A rough circle was formed, with my lord in the middle, around whom other torches burned, as further guests and servants arrived. So he waited, at the centre of the circle, weighing the apple in his hand, throwing it in the cold air, catching it, calling out his open challenge, saying, 'Who can keep this from me?'

He peered around him at the faces of his companions, lit by the light of the encircling flames. The guests and servants stared back at him, hoping for entertainment. Choosing his time, my lord threw the apple towards me.

In that moment, it seemed to me, time slowed. The cold air brought sobriety, lifting the fumes of the wine. Above me, the apple seemed no more than a star-gleam; then, falling towards me, it expressed its unexpected mass. I caught it as deftly as I could, surprised by the sudden weight of it, in my spare left hand – the one not holding a torch. Around me other hands applauded the speed of my catch.

My lord wiped his lips with the back of his wrist, flexed his shoulders, began his charge like a boar towards me. His speed and determination seemed almost devilish. I waited until he was almost upon me, then flicked the apple over his charging head, watching it sail through the air, upwards, glinting like a planet, until one of the sturdier servants caught it.

There was another burst of applause. With fearsome dexterity my lord turned and pursued the apple to its catcher. The same servant, holding the apple, appeared intimidated by his ferocious charge. Even so, he managed to throw it over his lordship's head in time. Another guest caught it. (And so it seemed to me that, as I watched the game, I observed the circle from above, the apple sailing through air, the scion of the house chasing with absorption and ferocity, almost under its shadow, panther-like, moving so fast from thrower to catcher that beneath each glimmering flight he seemed to be gaining ground on the flying prey.)

It happened that one of the greater guests, a powerful Seneschal, a renowned warrior, caught the apple a moment before the charging youth – closing on him at speed and calculating its upward trajectory – snatched it in the very act of rising again from his hand.

'Huzzah!' our host called out in triumph. Holding his prize aloft, he backed into the middle of the circle, to rising roars. There he took a wolf bite of the apple, to further approbation, while among the gathered others, I watched in smiling approval.

Chapter 4

MY LORD BURNED WITH A CONTINUOUS, dense energy. He was one of those who needed little sleep. When he rested, he slept instinctively and deeply, like an animal. After we had thrown the apple, he approached me and said, 'Master Shakespeare, I wish to speak with you about certain matters.'

It was already past midnight. In his chambers during the early hours, he paced up and down. I stood still and silent, leaning against the wall, not daring to interrupt his fervent movement. Eventually he turned towards me. 'Is Master Marlowe older than you?'

'Hardly,' I answered, surprised by this odd question. 'By only a few months, I believe.'

'Yet you openly acknowledge him your superior?'

'My superior in art,' I said. 'The worthier pen.'

'You say so freely.'

To which I answered, 'Every scribbler in our land is in debt to his great peroration, his mighty line. Where he leads, we others follow.'

'You truly admire *Faustus*?' he asked.

'Marlowe *is* Faustus,' I replied. 'They say he necromances spirits, that he is on speaking terms with Mephistopheles.'

He smiled at that, saying, 'This ... other work that you mentioned at our table –'

'*Hero and Leander*,' I said.

'*Hero and Leander*. What is it, precisely?'

'A poem about love, dwelling much on masculine beauty. It is said that he intends to dedicate it to you.'

His face lit up. He was addicted to praise.

'To me?'

'So it is said.'

'Yet it is unfinished.'

I smiled. 'So it is said.'

He looked at me searchingly. 'And you do not mind ... a rival for your praise?'

'He has a worthy subject.'

He paused and considered me. 'You are honest. You see coldly and clearly, and yet I believe you burn hot inside.'

I would not deny it. So before him I said, as though in affirmation of a fact, 'I see clearly and burn hot.'

That night, after I left my lord's rooms, I attempted to give some further shape to the thoughts I had earlier that day – that his youth and beauty incited dreams in the observer. Earlier that morning, when he emerged from the lake, there was one more witness than those I had already described. In the dawn mists, a figure was collecting brushwood in some dense, nearby scrub. At first I thought it might have been a boar, rooting in the undergrowth. Despite the low-lying vapour, I could begin to make out an elderly crone, bent-backed, in a grey hood. She had been dragging a sack of brushwood backwards from a thick covert where she had been collecting sticks for firewood.

The foliage was so dense there that it would have been difficult to lift the sack under the immediate oppression of the overhanging boughs. Once she was out of its entanglements, she intended to lift her load onto her shoulders. So she emerged from the thicket backwards, like some strange animal, hauling her load, wheezing and gasping, at precisely that place on the shore where my lord, unconscious of any other human witness, was approaching after his swim in the lake. I supposed that, suspecting a meeting, I could have warned her of his emergence from the water, but the comical nature of our situation touched me and stimulated my curiosity.

Perhaps the elderly crone heard the jingle of horses' bridles, or the splashing of my lord's feet as he neared the shore, for she seemed suddenly aware of others in her vicinity. She turned round, perplexed, and was faced with an entirely naked youth emerging like a god from the elements.

Her face, I do recall, was a picture. It was a wonderful old countenance, wrinkled and shriven, but with a clear, bright, and intelligent eye. I know enough of age to appreciate that the inhabiter of that bag of bones was the same being who had danced with graceful feet on the common in her youth.

For a brief moment her eye surveyed the figure that had risen from the waters – heavy, pale shoulders, long fair hair, the nub between the slender legs – with the purest appreciation.

Why should either of them have been offended? It is true that he, at first as startled as she, tensed a little from the unexpected meeting; but seeing almost immediately that his witness offered no offence and appeared appreciative of his form, he relaxed, and even lowered the lid of his eye in the form of a rakish wink. For a moment, all that old woman's Christmases seemed rolled into one. She cackled with pleasure, allowed her eye one more appreciative traverse of his figure, and then – modesty imposing itself at last – turned away to lift the sack onto her back. It seemed she shook with laughter as she slowly disappeared into the mist.

I handed my lord his clothes. When he had dressed, we rode back through the morning towards the great house.

Chapter 5

I HAD BEEN WORKING on the idea of composing a
sequence of poems or sonnets addressed to my patron.
The sonnet itself had a complex history. According to
a prevailing fashion, it was addressed by a poet to a mistress, often one who was out of reach, after whom he
yearned, or at least affected to do so for the sake of the
fulsome compliments he would bestow upon her. It was
a convention which had emerged in part at least from
the troubadour tradition of France, and since we English tended to ape French fashions, it had its adherents
amongst the nobility. Great ladies found it amusing to
be addressed thus, in appropriately lofty language, by

one who remained suitably distant and chaste. I had one obvious difficulty in my own circumstances: my patron was a master, not a mistress. Yet precisely because of this, the convention imposed its own interesting construction. It reminded me of the convention in a theatre, whereby a man would play a woman's role. By the same processes, perhaps, it stimulated rather than repressed the imagination.

If a man, rather than a woman, were to be the object of those high-flown praises, a more subtle tone was required – of fervent infatuation which was, at the same time, ironic. And since my master was himself both intelligent and someone who enjoyed praise, I began with the advantage of a most discerning subject for my poetry.

Until then I had mainly drafted certain thoughts in the form of individual lines and brief passages of description or argument. But now, reaching my rooms, I attempted to write a sonnet which would perhaps function as a keystone to my efforts. With a clean page before me, I began by praising my master's beauty as though he were my beloved mistress, at the same time asserting that my love was not physical, but spiritual.

A woman's face, with Nature's own hand painted,
Hast thou, the master-mistress of my passion;
A woman's gentle heart, but not acquainted
With shifting change, as is false women's fashion;
An eye more bright than theirs, less false in rolling,
Gilding the object whereupon it gazeth;
A man in hew all Hews in his controlling,
Which steals men's eyes, and women's souls amazeth.
And for a woman wert thou first created;
Till Nature, as she wrought thee, fell a-doting,
And by addition thee of me defeated,
By adding one thing to my purpose nothing.
*   But since she prick'd thee out for women's pleasure,*
*   Mine be thy love, and thy love's use their treasure.*

If it were a sonnet which would form the key to the others I would write, there were certain ways in which I would attempt to make it stand out from the other sonnets I intended to compose. I deliberately chose to use eleven syllables to the line, as opposed the usual ten. In addition, I left a clue to the identity of my patron in the phrase:

A man in hew all Hews in his controlling,

The mysterious word 'Hews', with a capital letter, as though it were a name, would be opaque to the merely casual reader. But since my patron was Henry Wriothesley, Earl of Southampton, whose initials were HWES, an anagram of Hews, it would give a clue to the identity of the fair young man. It happened too that certain of those tradesmen, builders and merchants who had cause to address my lord, or wrote him bills, often altered his name to 'Henry, Earl Wriothesley of Southampton'. Thus 'Hews' would act as a vernacular reference to my patron.

I chose the moment carefully to show the poem to my lord. We had been riding through the forest that early summer morning. He dismounted from his horse in order to walk to the edge of a nearby decline, so that he could survey the surrounding country. As I walked alongside him, I drew the paper forth from my clothes. Taking it from me, he read it with studied amusement. I watched him raise his eyebrows at the last few lines, read them again, and then laugh the louder.

'Most excellent,' he said. 'I am thy spiritual love,

but Nature pricked me out for women's pleasure.' He smiled again. 'I should be desirous to see more.'

I asked him whether he had noted the hidden reference to his name in 'Hews'.

My patron said, 'If these are dangerous times, as you counsel me, then it is right that living persons should not be mentioned. And since these are private poems, for our own enjoyment, Master Shakespeare, I believe all your references to me as your patron should be hidden to an outside view. If you will accept those conditions, pray continue as you will.'

He returned the paper to me. 'Will you make a copy of this, in your own hand, so that I may keep it?'

It became our custom. When I had finished a poem, I would copy it; keeping the overwritten and amended original for myself, giving the fair version to him. As for the content, perhaps I could do better in due course. But the tone – part infatuation, part irony, directed at a mysterious and unidentified beautiful youth – seemed well set for our enterprise. In due course I would arrange the poems in a different order, but meanwhile they would steadily accrue.

Chapter 6

THAT SUMMER, GRANTED MY LORD'S PERMISSION, I began to sing his praises in those effusive and extravagant terms so dearly beloved of my countrymen. For there was another circumstance which propelled me towards such orisons to beauty, and my lord towards receiving them with a good grace. It happened that in our kingdom we were ruled by a Queen, a veritable lion-hearted Empress, and in our pleading for her mercy and her favour we all of us sounded like troubadour poets singing of our love. It happened too that the very form or construction of my sonnets – soliciting the favours of a fair subject – rhymed with the prevailing fashion among courtiers. And so I proceeded from one to the next, gaining greater confidence as each one was well received by my patron.

When in disgrace with fortune and men's eyes,
I all alone beweep my outcast state,
And trouble deaf heaven with my bootless cries,
And look upon myself, and curse my fate,
Wishing me like to one more rich in hope,
Featur'd like him, like him with friends possess'd,
Desiring this man's art, and that man's scope,
With what I most enjoy contented least;
Yet in these thoughts myself almost despising,
Haply I think on thee, – and then my state,
Like to the lark at break of day arising
From sullen earth, sings hymns at heaven's gate;
 For thy sweet love remember'd such wealth brings,
 That then I scorn to change my state with kings.

I continued to sing my calculated songs throughout that summer, piling verse on verse, page on page, making each time a fresh copy for my lord. With the form established between us, I began to exceed myself

in gallantry, making the object of my praises the subject of love itself. Though my poem was addressed to a
handsome youth, I strove as best I could to reflect some
universal desire.

Shall I compare thee to a summer's day?
Thou art more lovely and more temperate:
Rough winds do shake the darling buds of May,
And summer's lease hath all too short a date:
Sometime too the eye of heaven shines,
And often is his gold complexion dimm'd;
And every fair from fair sometimes declines,
By chance, or nature's changing course, untrimm'd;
But thy eternal summer shall not fade,
Nor lose possession of that fair thou ow'st;
Nor shall Death brag thou wander'st in his shade,
When in eternal lines to time thou grow'st:
   So long as men can breathe, or eyes can see,
   So long lives this, and this gives life to thee.

I burnt my nightly hours as he inferred, confined to
my small room, bent over my formal rhythms, counting
the beats on my fingers, feeling for that thread of sense

which would hold together the discreet observations and soaring praises they would contain. Sometimes several days, or even a week, would pass without a single line that I deemed worth showing to him. At other times, in the course of a night's labour, I would find several pages of some worth had piled one upon the other. So, often laboriously and occasionally swiftly, I began to accumulate my efforts.

Who will believe my verse in time to come,
If it were fill'd with your most high deserts?
Though yet, heaven knows, it is but as a tomb
Which hides your life, and shows not half your parts.
If I could write the beauty of your eyes,
And in fresh numbers number all your graces,
The age to come would say, 'This poet lies;
Such heavenly touches ne'er touch'd earthly faces.'
So should my papers, yellow'd with their age,
Be scorn'd, like old men of less truth than tongue,
And your true rights be term'd a poet's rage
And stretched metre of an antique song:
   But were some child of yours alive that time,
   You should live twice, – in it and in my rhyme.

The introduction of a child of his own making who would perpetuate that beauty was accidental and felicitous, though perhaps with my poetic senses now attuned to his particular circumstances, I presaged some future development.

Chapter 7

THERE WERE TIMES when my lord seemed to regard me with a certain wry amusement for my pains. In conversation one day, he deliberately switched the subject from the sonnet he had been reading towards another subject perhaps closer to his heart. At the time he was staring at the floor, as though gathering his thoughts. Now he turned to peer once more at me with his green eyes, flecked with gold. 'My mother has spoken to you again?'

'She has.'

'And on the usual subject?'

'The usual,' I said.

'And you take her side, as always.'

'Her side is your side,' I replied, and added, 'She speaks for you.'

He turned away. 'Damn me, if she does.'

I said, 'There are matters which await you. That is all she says.'

'Yes, yes, matters!' This was fierce and fast. He seemed compelled to continue, for the rest of what he wished to say now streamed forth. 'It is time, perhaps, that you knew something further of me, of my closer circumstances ... '

'Your closer circumstances?' The phrase rang oddly, and I was at a loss as to this new departure.

He said, 'You know, for example, that my father died when I was eight.' I nodded, nervous at his apparent continued excitation. Now, with an effort, he seemed to compose himself sufficiently to explain. 'After my father had been buried, my Lord Burghley became my legal guardian. When I was still no more than a child, my great guardian caused me to sign a contract, promising to marry his granddaughter, Elizabeth de Vere, on pain of which refusal, on reaching my majority, I would pay a fine – a terrible fine, almost equal to the value of my entire estate. You know of this?'

It was common gossip, so I said, cautiously, 'I have heard rumours, nothing more.'

'Then,' he insisted, 'you have heard of the disposition of my Lord Burghley?'

I said only that I knew that he had the disposition of a lawyer, and the reputation of a courtier.

'And what else have you heard of him?' he asked.

'That he is our Queen's closest advisor, and the strongest voice in the Privy Council.'

'Yes, yes, that is his political suit. But have you ever seen the man, in person?'

'No, my lord.'

'He is the coldest creature that ever walked upon this earth. He regards all art, all painting, all poetry, as vanity. The theatre in particular he considers both impious and seditious. They say he is not of the Puritan party, yet he has a puritan's instincts. Whatever he touches, becomes ice. If he walks through summer, winter follows. And yet it was he who replaced my dead and lamented father – *in nomine patris.*'

'In your maturity,' I tentatively suggested, 'You will grow away from him.'

'If only it were so!' He seemed a little calmer now, staring at the floor, but still biting his fist, his attention set in some other realm. 'Even from a distance, from London, he still controls my household. My mother too is fearful of him.'

'Why, my lord?' I asked.

He raised his eyes again to mine. 'If I do not marry the one he has chosen for me, my mother too shall be ruined by the catastrophic fine that my Lord Burghley, in his wisdom, shall apportion on me.'

He remained unusually excited. I did my best to calm him, saying, 'Your mother thinks more of an heir from you than of your inheritance.'

'Yes, yes! He blackmails her too, though at a remove. His reach is great. His claws are in everyone.'

I was about to say something more, but my lord continued, 'And then, of course, there is my tutor, Master Florio.' He paused, raised his eyes towards the ceiling, adding with emphasis, '*Master Florio.*'

I attempted emollience. 'Master John Florio. A

most eminent Italian scholar, to whom you owe your own achievement in learning.'

'A fine tutor, and in that respect I perhaps am willing to accept your description. But we should not forget one thing – that he writes regularly to his own master.'

'His own master?'

'My Lord Burghley, who appointed him.'

I halted, silenced in part by the strange complexity of my patron's circumstances. 'Perhaps he writes to apprise my Lord Burghley of your great advances in learning.'

He laughed at this, with a dismissive air. 'No, no, my dear Master William. He writes of my predisposition to marriage, of my carousing in certain company. And so, Master Florio, instructed by his master, admonishes me for my behaviour. Amongst his lessons he coldly arranges certain threats against me. Why, the man's an Italian, of passionate mind. Yet he passes on the current of my Lord Burghley's coldness as though it were his own.'

I smiled at this, and said, 'Machiavelli too was a Florentine,' then added, 'In Master Florio's favour, he imposes upon himself the same discipline he would exert upon you.'

'What discipline is that?' he shot back at me.

'He constructs a dictionary of Italian and English, a great and noble undertaking – '

'In his own interest – '

'And in my interests, too,' I said, 'for I find in his other translations of Italian works a rich source of stories and quaint dramas. It is, I admit, my own concern, but he is generous to me with his translations – '

'And no doubt you are grateful to him, as you should be. And I am grateful to him, too. But why should a man play double if he is, as you say, of so single a mind? Why should he serve two masters if one master is enough?'

'It sounds as though his other master – my Lord Burghley – is difficult to refuse.'

'Don't you see? He admires his master, just as Signor Machiavelli admired his prince ... ' He paused, then burst out, '*He is Lord Burghley's flea!*'

I allowed the first clean wave of his anger to pass me by, swiftly and uncomfortably. 'How can you be certain that what he writes is anything more than praise of you? You yourself received your Master's degree from Cambridge at the age of sixteen. He has good reason to be proud of his pupil.'

But he objected, 'You are too generous. You take every other's part. I believe you' – he struggled for words – 'complicate matters.'

'My lord, it is in my nature to seek for wider motive.'

'Then, speaking of wider motive, let us return to my mother. She would arrange some further slip of a girl to marry me, and because I hesitate – '

'She would accept your direct refusal,' I said. 'If you proposed another match – '

He turned away in anger. 'Another girl, another victim of the great imperative ... ' His voice became fierce again, ironical. '*Why, marry and produce an heir.*'

I could not help but smile at his retort.

'You laugh at me, Master William?' he asked.

I replied, as gently as I could, 'No, sir, I do not laugh. I merely play the devil's advocate, as you have asked.'

He considered me for several moments. Who knows what he saw, or for what he searched. Perhaps he observed something genuine in my perplexity.

Calmer now, he appeared to ease a little. He said, 'I am not like you, William – so silent, so determined upon your life. You resemble nothing so much as one of those steel springs inside a lock. Tonight I will go to bed and sleep, and dream. And you, to some further vigil at the board?'

It was true. I observed in my mind's eye another appointment, until the early dawn, with a sheet of paper and the little flame. 'That is how I choose to burn my hours.'

'Yet it is I who have no other cause, more weighty than to be myself.'

I said, as gently as I could, 'That is enough.'

'Oh, it would be,' he said, 'if I knew the meaning of myself.'

'You will learn it.'

'How?' he asked, with genuine puzzlement.

I smiled at his earnestness. 'It will grow into you. You will grow into it.'

'Will I?'

'You will.'

'You make a pun upon your name.'

'You made it first. I merely follow you. Your will is your own.'

'Damn these circumstances, though. In many respects you are kindness itself. Yet still you press me.'

'I do not press you. I remind you.'

'Of my duty.'

'Of yourself.'

'And you will teach me to be myself?'

'I will attempt to remind you, from time to time, of what you may be.'

Chapter 8

*B*UT OUR RELATIONS WERE SUCH that my patron was apt to remind me of what I should be, too. One day while out riding, he said, 'I should like to show you at first hand how my Lord Burghley attempts to influence me. Two years ago, when I was merely seventeen years, my guardian engaged one of his secretaries, a Master John Clapham, to write a poem in Latin, dedicated to me, called *Narcissus*.'

'A poem called *Narcissus*?' I was incredulous, I must admit. Rumours had moved around him, suggesting vanity, but here was a source of its direct propagation by an interested party. Even then, I could not help but smile. I had a vision of some ambitious young secretary, at the behest of his master, scratching out a poem in orotund Latin, addressed to a youth who would not obey the dictums of his enraged protector.

From the depths of his clothes my patron withdrew a large, portentous document that seemed almost like a will or testament. He said, 'I have brought it for you to consider. An entire poem which urges me, in formal Latin, to cease from my vain preoccupations with myself. Its clear implication is that I should marry the young woman who waits so patiently and unhappily for me.'

My consternation that such a poem had been written was due, in part at least, to my patron's assertion that his guardian despised art. Perhaps I began to see a little more deeply into Lord Burghley's soul. Art was permissible if it served a political purpose, and especially if it served his own. Setting these thoughts aside, I said, 'The poem mentions you directly?'

'No, not in so many words. It is dedicated to me, but it extemporises *ad infinitum* on a young man who might be thought to resemble me.'

'Why did the poet – my Lord Burghley's secretary – not have the courage of his convictions, and make you its direct subject?'

He laughed. 'For good reason. The poem is happy enough to omit certain details of my circumstances – that the marriage contract was signed when I was a child, before I had even met my intended, or that she is the granddaughter of my guardian, so that the person who will benefit from the arrangement is my Lord Burghley.'

'I shall look forward to studying it,' I said, accepting the proffered document from his hand. A question struck me. 'Are there others such as you for whom Lord Burghley acts as guardian?'

I witnessed a somewhat rueful smile. 'It seems that, as a reward for his continuing labours for Her Majesty, for some twenty years my Lord Burghley has held the position of Master of the Court of Wards. All those infants and children who inherit large estates and who lose their father are placed in his care. It would seem to be a habit of my guardian to contract his wards to an approved marriage which benefits him. If they refuse, the marriage contract will place such a heavy fine upon them that their estate will pass to him or his chosen beneficiaries in perpetuity.'

I had a vision of my Lord Burghley – industrious, cold, puritanical – exploiting the properties of small and defenceless children, offering them the choice of unhappiness in an arranged marriage – or, as an alternative, if they did not obey him, an impoverishment of their birthright.

As though my patron understood the line and direction of my thought, he said, 'My guardian has used his position to make himself one of the richest men in the land. Amongst his many properties, he has built a magnificent palace for himself at Theobalds, and another great house in Covent Garden.'

We rode on in silence for a while. Mulling over my patron's account of his arranged marriage, I became curious as to whether he and his betrothed had ever met.

He smiled at my enquiry. 'When I was old enough to consider more seriously the fate which had been arranged for me, I took it upon myself to travel to my betrothed's parents' house with the intention of meeting her, and making her acquaintance. Lord Burghley's daughter Ann had married the Earl of Oxford, Edward de Vere. My betrothed, Elizabeth de Vere, was the product of their marriage. Perhaps I was foolish in announcing my visit beforehand. My betrothed's parents, when I entered their house, hid her from me. At first they told me she was unwell, and indisposed to a meeting. Perhaps they hoped that my patience would wear thin and I would depart. I began to perceive that their daughter's own voluntary acquiescence in the marriage was something to be doubted, but this only redoubled my determination. In the circumstances, I was forced to wait impatiently for several days. Eventually, out of persistence, I was permitted to meet my intended.'

'You spoke with your betrothed?'

'During the meeting, she was not even permitted to speak to me directly. Any question I might put to her, however courteous, her mother answered on her behalf. It was only by accident that one day, while I walked in the grounds of the house, in the greatest perplexity at my predicament, I caught sight of my betrothed in a distant part of the garden. She was seated on a bench, attended by her elderly nurse. I made my way there as quickly and discreetly as I was able. The beldame, who at first was inclined to keep me at bay, took pity on two such youthful creatures, and allowed us to converse in a private corner of a nearby arbour, while she kept a nervous watch.'

I was fascinated by the oddness of the arrangement – the image of two youthful creatures sworn to each other against their will, for the greed or benefit of others. I could not help but compare it with my own marriage, to a woman eight years older than me, my own Anne Hathaway, and with the fact that our own marriage ceremony was arranged somewhat in haste on account of her pregnancy.

My curiosity led me to enquire, 'You were not drawn by affection towards your betrothed?'

He smiled. 'From what I saw of her, I believe I could have liked her, but I do not love her or feel any special affection for her. Yet I found that she too, once allowed to express herself, had an independent disposition. And in the course of our conversation I discovered that she felt nothing but sympathy for me about my own predicament. It seemed that in her heart my intended was as set against marrying me by arrangement as I was against marrying her.'

'So you found yourselves in cautious agreement?'

He smiled. 'It was a strangely happy meeting. When two people find something in common, it often happens that a bond of sympathy forms between them. We were able to talk only briefly, because the beldame was growing nervous that some other party might observe us in discussion. When the old woman saw my betrothed's mother emerge from the house to look for her daughter, she fell into a panic, and insisted that we two should separate immediately.'

'Yet it seems you and your betrothed parted on amicable terms.'

'Before I slipped away, my intended said she would write to her grandfather, Lord Burghley, complaining, in courteous terms, that some account of her own feelings should be taken in the matter.' He smiled again. 'I should like to have seen the letter.'

I looked at the sheaf of pages he had given me, each covered in a neat but somewhat laboured hand, and carefully placed it in my own clothes for safekeeping.

That night, seated at my board, I studied the poem more carefully. My own grammar-school Latin was rigorous enough to enable me to get at the meaning. I had been trained in rhetoric, in study of the Latin masters such as Ovid, Terence, Mantuan, Tully, Horace, Sallust. But where once, in my younger days, I had been more than capable of discriminating between various styles, and imitating them, in my life as a player I had forgotten some of the finer points of the Latin verse I had studied in my youth.

Even so, I could see in the poem before me that although the Latin itself was grammatical enough, the verses themselves were the most lamentable doggerel it had ever been my misfortune to read. Conceit after laboured conceit rolled forth ceaselessly, mixed with wooden references to a vague, mythological past which was imperfectly and hastily resurrected for the purposes of the present. I had a vision of Lord Burghley poring over this work in progress, nodding his sage head in approval at the sentiments, perhaps inserting a phrase of his own here or there in order to strengthen a point – since it is ever the view of those in authority that they are superior in art over those who merely write.

As I endeavoured to understand the meanings and conceits, smiling to myself at the clumsy metaphors and plodding locutions, I believed I could even perceive in certain places the interdiction of Lord Burghley's hand – in the form of a sharper phrase here or an argument there. In the young scribe's attempts at rhetoric there was at least a certain heartfelt attempt at metre and rhythm, though when clearly overlain by his master's instructions and interpolations the verse was utterly devoid of any music.

There is nothing that I enjoy more than 'turning' a work to new advantage. I wondered whether I could satirise the earnest homilies in *Narcissus*. Since my desire was to entertain my patron, I could perhaps accept in light-hearted fashion the charge of narcissism on his behalf. But instead of arguing that his youthful self-absorption was the enemy of propagation, I would continue to sing that the very beauty of my patron was the chief reason why he should reproduce himself and perpetuate his line.

Several nights later, with the laboured conceits of *Narcissus* still echoing in my mind, I began to draft a poem on the subject which, though it lacked the usual formal precision at which I aimed, nevertheless expressed the sincerity of my anger. The first draft ran:

Lord of laughter, you showed me Narcissus,
A poem whose heart is hollowed by power;
Falsely addressed, it pretends to kiss us,
Telling of beauty, Cupid's sweet bower;
Yet cold hearts form cold minds, eyes lose their sight;
Stealing our childhood, it counsels good faith.
Framed by deceit, the sun's fatal glower
Reversing all virtue, makes permanent night.
In hell's own smithies, Authority labours,
Shadow on shadow, reversing the year;
And what is more wretched, than making wretched,
When, lacking all mercy, he sheds no tear?
   Then punish him not for what he may say;
   A mind without light can never see day.

I showed the poem to my patron while we were out riding. He read it carefully as his horse walked companionably alongside mine. Raising his eye from the page he laughed out aloud in fierce delight. 'A most sincere and clear castigation of my Lord Burghley.' But when his mirth had subsided, he added, 'That is its virtue, but also its danger.' As though demonstrating his own skill at recalling, my patron read the poem to himself a second time, raised his face into the sunlight and, without a prompt, repeated the entire work verbatim. It was a feat of repetition which even I, an actor, could appreciate. But then, having memorised the poem, he touched his forehead lightly with his forefinger, and said, 'It is better preserved in here.' Saying this, he proceeded to tear the page into a dozen small pieces. At the same time he said, 'If this were to fall into the hands of Lord Burghley's spies, and my guardian were to set eyes upon it, you may be certain he would order a warrant for your arrest on the charge of sedition.'

I observed the pieces drift down to the surface of the stream along whose banks we rode, and settle there.

I said, 'I have not named my Lord Burghley directly.'

'You have named the poem he authorised,' my patron replied. 'That is enough, since it carries his imprimatur. Furthermore, he would prosecute you for also naming Authority in the abstract and attempting to undermine her. I believe, sir, that in these times your well-being, and perhaps your life, would be forfeit within a few months of his taking sight of any such document.'

I watched the pieces float on the stream and observed how the fingers of paper, becoming water-logged, slowly began to sink into the river's darker depths. As though interrupting my contemplation, my lord said, 'My dear Master Shakespeare, you are my mentor in art and in life, but in politics, I believe I have certain things to teach you. From this day onward, I most earnestly hope that everything you write in your sonnets should be couched in ambiguity. Your hiding place should be language itself. If you are ever arraigned or indicted for your works, your defence must be that every word or phrase of yours may be capable of a different interpretation, or may be viewed in a different light.'

'You forbid me to address any matters politic?'

'No, that is my point. With regard to my Lord Burghley, or other matters of high authority, I advise you merely to hide your direct meaning.'

'Even though it places a severe constraint on the writing?'

'There is no restriction that cannot be overcome with subtlety,' he said. 'Ambivalence of meaning is a gift of yours. It must become not merely a clever conceit, but the source of your future safety.'

'Now you lecture me on my nature,' I replied, 'as I lectured you on yours.'

'Precisely so. Any poem of yours which moves, by aberration, into perfect clarity, I will attempt to persuade you to censor, for your own sake.'

I absorbed the weight of this peroration. But a part of me was still disturbed by his peremptory action. I said, 'I believe that Master Marlowe would have openly authored that poem.'

My patron smiled. 'It is in Marlowe's nature to

challenge all who pose in authority. He lives by his own calling. But you, sir, should aim to preserve yourself for as long as you may. Only live birds sing.'

'Only ambiguous birds, it seems,' I said, a part of me still stinging with mortification at the loss of my draft.

Chapter 9

My wounded feelings at his treatment of my poem were not long-lived. As my hurt cooled, I began to see the sense of my patron's objection. He had permitted me to write verses praising him in exaggerated and ironic terms, and had cautioned me in favour of complex ambivalence for my own protection. The thought occurred to me, not for the first time, that what at first appears a restraint may also be a spur to greater invention.

There had been an example of it in my own work. In the English language the pattern of speech settles almost naturally into the double beat, the iamb – a short beat followed by a longer beat, *di dah*. In my plays, following Marlowe, I had used five of these iambs to make up a line, the iambic pentameter, containing ten syllables. My sonnets were also predominantly ten syllables, but differed in having a rhyming scheme at the end of each line. Before attempting a sonnet I should have believed my sonnets' usual rhyme scheme of alternative lines, ending on a rhyming couplet, would have restricted the composition and rendered it more difficult. But on those quiet vigils when I worked at the board, as often as not the rhyme itself would suggest the next sentence, and so what seemed at first an impediment was transformed into a source of invention.

Meanwhile, I transmitted my anger at my patron's treatment by his guardian into more abstract form:

> *Tir'd with all these, for restful death I cry*
> *As to behold desert a beggar born,*
> *And needy nothing trimm'd in jollity,*
> *And purest faith unhappily forsworn,*
> *And gilded honour shamefully misplaced,*
> *And maiden virtue rudely strumpeted,*

And right perfection wrongfully disgraced,
And strength by limping sway disabled,
And art made tongue-tied by authority,
And folly – doctor-like – controlling skill,
And simple truth miscall'd simplicity,
And captive good attending captain ill:
   Tir'd with all these, from these would I be gone,
   Save that, to die, I leave my love alone.

My patron had requested me to be ambivalent, and no doubt would be appreciative of my listing of the catalogue of calumny directed against him and his reputation. But since he was a remarkably perceptive and intelligent soul, he would have noticed in the line: '*And art made tongue-tied by authority*', an ambiguous reference to a certain incident of tearing up one of my sonnets and allowing the pieces to drift down onto the surface of the river. Yet, in his favour, I would be foolish to deny that a part of my joy in labouring at my verses for one such as he, who was so confident in his own sincerity, was that he would appreciate subtle irony at his own expense.

So I continued to work upon my sonnets in earnest,

turning and re-directing the intended meaning of *Narcissus*, labouring during the night hours at my board, producing one paean to my patron after another. And in the process of committing myself to my labours, I began to fall in love not so much with the idealised creature I addressed there as with the form of the sonnet itself – that almost perfect amalgamation of precise structure and living animate being.

The process of writing even a single sonnet was a difficult and demanding performance. Often I would toil with little or no result. Yet sometimes, in the course of my labours, a line or phrase, emerging from shadowy intuition, would appear beneath my pen, and in a trance of concentration I would examine its unexpected beauty. Perhaps paradoxically, it was only when such a phrase or line was written down that I could view it from every angle, considering it for its hidden beauties and ambiguities. Sometimes, because I mistrusted my judgement in the full heat of invention, I would set aside a poem and take it out later, on another occasion, when I was more able to peruse with a cold and objective eye the deeper meaning of what I had written. At other times, sensing some imminent victory, I would press ahead, like a horseman leaping an obstacle without knowing what lay on the other side. When I asserted there was something animate in the sonnet, during the height of composition it seemed to me that I was controlling a living creature in almost a literal manner, a being whose inner life required all my wit and attention to give it its proper form and motion.

Sometimes these imaginings, far from granting me sleep, pursued me to my narrow cot, where I lay sleepless while my mind brimmed with thoughts and images. Partly for the entertainment of my patron, I recorded my nightly obsessions with my labours:

> *Weary with toil, I haste me to my bed,*
> *The dear repose for limbs with travel tired;*
> *But then begins a journey in my head,*
> *To work my mind, when body's work's expir'd:*
> *For then my thoughts – from far where I abide –*
> *Intend a zealous pilgrimage to thee,*
> *And keep my drooping eyelids open wide,*
> *Looking on darkness which the blind do see:*
> *Save that my soul's imaginary sight*
> *Presents thy shadow to my sightless view,*

Which, like a jewel hung in ghostly night,
Makes black night beauteous and her old face new.
  Lo! thus by day my limbs, by night my mind,
  For thee, and for myself no quiet find.

Chapter 10

THERE WAS ANOTHER PRESENCE in that great house, one who hardly stirred from his rooms because of his labours, whose wife and several children I had seen mostly at a distance. The following day, I knocked upon his heavy door with its brass knocker. From inside a voice marked with an Italian accent rang out. 'Who calls?'

'Shakespeare!' I responded.

Sounds of footsteps followed across the floor, both impatient and dragging, as though it might be a wounded beast, or as if he were lugging some imperishable weight. With an aggravated growl, a wooden bar was swung aside. The oak door widened and grinned open.

Facing me was a tall, thin man in his late forties; scholarly, intense, with fierce and brooding eyes. His harried gaze fixed on mine.

'Master Shakespeare, the poet,' he announced. There was something cynical, both agitated and mocking, about his demeanour.

'Master Florio, the scholar,' I replied. 'I shamelessly seek a volume to study.'

'Which volume, now?' He examined me. 'Speak, if you dare.'

'Why, a volume of your own fine work. Who else's?'

Master Florio smiled at my importunity, but relented. As though quoting some private text, he said to himself, 'Thou art a flatterer.' To which I said, 'No better and no worse.'

He stood aside and let me pass. Inside the sullen gloom his rooms were a scholar's den, with manuscripts piled high on chests and chairs. The remaining furniture was submerged beneath piles of written documents.

He glanced around at this confusion with something like approval, and said, 'You seek inspiration for your verses? You wish to rob my resources for your own?'

'Precisely, sir,' I said. 'Most ably put.'

He smiled again at my audacity, seating himself once more at his desk. He waved his hand in the general direction of the small back room where he stored his works. 'You may look through my volumes. But in return for my generosity, you will forgive me if I continue with my labours.'

I bowed. 'You are kindness itself.'

He called for his wife, pronouncing 'Lucia' in the Italian manner. A door opened and a handsome dark-haired woman appeared, in her middle twenties, with a small child held on her hip.

'Lucia,' my host repeated. 'Show Master Shakespeare to the little cell.'

In answer to his instruction, Lucia nodded. She set down the child, turned and led me through a bedchamber strewn with children's clothes, opening another door. There I found a tiny cell with a single window, piled high with so many volumes it was almost impossible to stand.

She waited behind me, and said, 'It is not very inviting, sir.'

'Oh, it is inviting to me, madam.'

I noticed a volume that interested me and pulled it down from a high pile of books, blowing dust off it as I did so. '*The Discourses*, by Signor Niccolò Machiavelli,' I said. 'You have read him?'

She hovered in the doorway. 'I was told he was an evil man.'

'Evil? No. A sweet and kind man. But he who advises tyrants must place himself in the tyrant's mind.' Saying this, I could not help but think of her husband in the next room.

'That was his sin?' she asked, inquisitive. 'Placing himself in another's mind?'

'Sympathy was his sin, madam. Honesty and lucidity were his means. Peaceful governance was his intention.'

She half smiled at these unfamiliar descriptions. 'My husband says – '

But I was swift to intercept. 'Your husband is Signor Machiavelli's countryman, madam. In such matters he is like all of us; when we consider our close compatriots, we underrate our native genius.'

74

She contemplated this, and smiled. 'No man is a prophet in his own land.'

'Exactly so.' And so she disappeared, nodding and closing the door.

I found myself alone in that monk's cell, surrounded by books. But I was happy enough, sniffing the scents of ancient wisdom. Balancing Signor Machiavelli upon a high pile of other works, I leaned against the nearby wall and began to read, running the tips of my careful fingers along the page, mouthing the words as I concentrated on the line.

That evening I sat at my board with the intention to address a certain theme in a sonnet. Though it was summer, the clear nights dissipated heat. For warmth, I had gathered around my shoulders the pelt of a sheep. Beside me, a single candle guttered and shed a faint light.

Since my lord's full name was Henry Wriothesley, Earl of Southampton and Baron of Titchfield, some consideration was commonly made for the difficulty of pronunciation of his family name. For greater ease, even on formal occasions, Wriothesley was pronounced 'Rye-ose-ley', though it was more common still to pronounce it 'Rosely'. The combination of 'Rose' in the pronunciation of his name, and the heraldic roses which decorated his house, tempted me to compose on the subject of roses in my verse.

I scratched with a quill on a sheet of parchment, paused, counted beats on my fingers, mouthed a phrase silently to myself, put quill to paper, withdrew, hesitated, and wrote:

> *From fairest creatures we desire increase,*
> *That thereby beauty's Rose might never die,*

The poem began to take a clearer shape:

> *From fairest creatures we desire increase,*
> *That thereby beauty's Rose might never die,*
> *But as the riper should by time decease,*
> *His tender heir might bear his memory:*
> *But thou, contracted to thine own bright eyes,*
> *Feed'st thy light's flame with self-substantial fuel,*
> *Making a famine where abundance lies,*
> *Thyself thy foe, to thy sweet self too cruel.*

76

The following day, in the rose garden, I watched my lord mime the beat and then express aloud the final words:

Thou that art now the world's fresh ornament
And only herald to the gaudy spring,
Within thine own bud buriest thy content
And, tender churl, mak'st waste in niggarding.
Pity this world, or else this glutton be,
To eat the world's due, by the grave and thee.

Reclining on a bench in that walled garden in the sunlight, having finished the sonnet, he raised his attention from the page and whispered to himself, 'Damn me, it's beautiful.'

Seated opposite him, my back against a wall, I inclined my head in acknowledgement. He stretched out his arms in languor, speaking with the rasp of sleepiness, 'Yet you do my mother's bidding, and chide me again for not marrying.'

I nodded.

He raised his face to the warm sunlight, and

appeared to be thinking, for his eyelids fluttered. Then he opened his eyes, as though caught with an idea. 'Yet still, if my childlessness inspires such verse – why then, it must be continued!'

Something of his fire spread to me. I responded warmly to the idea, like a tutor to a favourite pupil. 'A fine conceit.'

My lord, charged with enthusiasm for his own idea, rose to his feet, and began walking up and down in an agitated state. 'So, then, let us have some more verses on this subject. Why, I believe I shall be angry if you do not pile more chastisement on my state. And if you do not chide me, sir, be certain that it will be I who chides you, for not doing your sacred duty.'

That night, seated in front of the board that served as my writing desk, I paused again. Beside me, the window was open. In the cool, starlit night I could hear a dog barking, and, further away, the scream of a vixen. I hesitated on my bench, whispered something to myself, and began again to scratch the surface of the paper with my quill.

When forty winters shall besiege thy brow,
And dig deep trenches in thy beauty's field,
Thy youth's proud livery, so gaz'd on now,
Will be a tatter'd weed, of small worth held:
Then, being asked where all thy beauty lies,
Where all the treasure of thy lusty days;
To say within thine own deep-sunken eyes,
Were an all-eating shame and shiftless praise.

The room seemed to become darker as I, engrossed in my own labour, set down the remainder of the poem, working as fast as I could, attempting to pin the thought like a live thing to the page. At times the poem seemed to draw away from me, and my corrections and crossings-out filled the page. For some time I worked, in a trance of concentration, until the sonnet was complete. Afterwards I stood at the small window of my cell, breathless, as though my mind had been voided by the effort. The following day, I listened while my lord completed the lines.

How much more praise deserv'd thy beauty's use,
If thou could answer, 'This fair child of mine
Shall sum my count, and make my old excuse,'
Proving his beauty by succession thine!
This were to be new-made when thou art old,
And see thy blood warm when thou feel'st it cold.

We were seated in our usual place in the garden, a corner protected from the prevailing winds. My lord set down the page he had been reading on the grass beside him. Folding his hands behind his head, he addressed the air above him. 'Such felicity! I believe you should show both of these sonnets to my mother. She will be forever in your debt for chastising me so ... beautifully.'

I remember looking about me, over the garden walls at the summer woods behind, at the country with its rolling meadows and woodlands, its nearby silver stream.

Observing my attention, my lord said, 'The colours of autumn already fall upon us. Soon it will be winter.'

I looked upwards and around me, at sunlight slanting through the nearby elms. Perhaps the beauty made my lord talkative; after gazing around at the country-side, he said, 'If I were without my duties, I should like, above everything, to return to my cell in St John's, in Cambridge, and burn candles and read volumes of Latin and Greek.'

'You do not fear solitude?'

He smiled. 'The greatest solitude I feel is when my relations are gathered at Christmas feast-day, and as the head of the family, and heir, I must act as *paterfamilias*. That is what I fear most – what is owed to others. Why, I prefer my books.' He looked up at the falling sunlight. 'You do not believe me?'

'Oh, I believe you, my lord. I believe every word you say.'

He gave me a strange look. 'Perhaps you do. Yet you smile.'

'I smile because I should like nothing more than to be in the bosom of my family.'

'Your family?' he asked.

'In Stratford,' I replied. 'I should like above all to sit at the head of the table, and carve the meat.'

He smiled, but he insisted, 'And yet you live in

exile, in a cold room, in my house in Hampshire, and seem to ask for nothing in the way of comfort except a supply of ink and parchment.'

'You misunderstand me, I think, if you believe I complain about my lot. I am a player and a scribbler, freely chosen.'

'You do yourself a disservice,' he said. 'You are called by some a great poet. You have dedicated both *Venus and Adonis* and *The Rape of Lucrece* to me. I have seen your worth.'

'I have also been called an upstart crow, who can hardly beat out a verse. And here I am, exiled from London by the plague, twice removed from that simple life that I desire.'

'We strike a melancholy note, between us. I wish to be a monk, and you –'

'To plunge myself into simple, unthinking human life.'

If he seemed amused by my earnestness, it was fleeting. 'I believe that in our aims, we swim past each other like fishes. I should give an arm to be like you –'

'Like me?'

He seemed to choose his words. 'Detached from this world, yet always observing.'

'And I should give an arm to be like you.'

'And what is that?' he asked. 'What does it mean "to be like me"?'

I struggled for expression. 'Living and breathing the world's rich scents.'

There was a moment's silence between us, after which he said, with a sigh, as though contemplative, 'My mother continues to instruct you regarding my behaviour?'

I nodded.

He smiled. 'I believe my mother would gladly exchange you for me.'

'Why so?' I asked.

'She admires your sober devotion to your work, and contrasts it with my dissipation and irresponsibility.'

I said, 'She loves you entirely and magnificently.'

'Not for myself, though. For what I owe. For what I should be.'

I did not comment. We considered peaceably the sloping shadows of the trees.

Chapter 11

THE FOLLOWING MORNING I leaned against a wall in the anteroom of my lord's mother, the Countess, staring out of the window at the autumn day.

The door to her room opened. I had expected her to open it herself, but instead her bailiff, a heavyset man, walked out carrying a bundle of sealed letters. His somewhat ursine body and short legs gave his gait a distinctive roll. Halting before me, he said, 'Master Shakespeare?'

I bowed my head indulgently.

'Her Ladyship would see you,' he said. 'She expects you.'

I thanked him. When he had passed on his way I walked towards the door of the inner chamber and knocked. Soft footsteps approached from the inside. The latch was raised soundlessly, the wood swung back. My lady was still strikingly beautiful.

'Master Shakespeare,' she said.

I bowed my head again, with greater sincerity than to her bailiff.

She drew back and I entered the room. Closing the door, she turned towards me, leaning upon it. 'My son sends me your verses.'

'They are nothing, madam. Sonnets merely.'

'Yet he commends you on your worth.'

'He is my patron, madam. In these hard times I am doubly grateful.'

'The London theatres are still closed by plague?'

'Except for a brief month at midwinter, my lady, when the cold seems to damp the fever. And then the entertainments are nothing more than masques and pantomimes.'

She hesitated. Her next statement seemed carefully framed. 'I hear you see much of my son.'

'He flatters me with his companionship.'

'His companionship?' She seemed to muse upon the word. There was a change of tone, a kind of insistence. 'You see much of him?'

Her question caused me to pause, to consider the weight of implication.

'Come now, Master Shakespeare,' the Countess said. 'It is time we discussed these matters. I do not hold it against you if you speak your mind. I am a woman with experience of this world.'

Perhaps something of the shock at such direct questioning showed on my face. I began, 'Madam, it is not my nature – '

'To be so disposed,' she said, 'towards young men?'

'No,' I answered. She considered me carefully, without speaking. Then she smiled ruefully. 'I do believe you … Yet he has other companions who … are so disposed.'

'Feckless youth, madam,' I responded. 'Puppies in a litter. You will not hold that against him.'

'Well turned, sir. He will not marry, though. You do not think these things are … related?'

I am not as bold as Marlowe, perhaps, but in the theatre I am used to a certain latitude in human affairs, so that sometimes I am driven to express an imp of general truth. 'Madam, if I may speak for myself, and with utmost sincerity, I see no connection between the quality of a man's soul and the private uses to which he puts his body.'

I saw a sudden blaze of feeling behind her eyes, but could not tell whether it was disapproval, or some other, more complex, emotion. Before her husband died, there had been a great scandal, in which he had accused his long-suffering wife of adultery, apparently without reason; but her blameless life as a widow since his early death seemed to have allayed the ghost of that accusation. She approached me now across the room. It was almost as though she dared me to proceed further with my thoughts. Under that impassioned gaze, it occurred to me that she was not so much questioning my words as testing my own sincerity.

'Continue, sir,' she said, as though challenging me.

'I merely apply my general beliefs to a singular matter,' I replied.

If she seemed to disapprove of my homily, it was

alleviated at least by a trace of humour. 'I sometimes forget, sir, that you are from the theatre.'

'Indeed, madam,' I replied.

'Where women are played by principal boys.'

'There are not many puritans on the stage, madam, I willingly concede.'

'Is that so? They do not gather there?'

'It is true, madam, that I have not seen many puritans clustering thickly in the theatre.'

Any amusement at my response seemed to occur entirely in her eyes, if it occurred at all. Since she continued to consider me directly, for my part I would continue to press my small advantage. Attempting to ameliorate, I said, 'Your son may sow wild oats, madam. But he is not idle.'

'Idle?'

'His tutors speak of a most gifted mind. He has the discipline of a scholar. And all who see him joust and play know that he has the frame and determination of a warrior.'

'Scholar and warrior,' she said, as if with disapproval, though she seemed a little more composed. 'Mere occupations. This house needs an heir.'

She turned away. Now it was my concern to choose my words carefully. 'I believe he has a fine and generous soul, madam. He will not disgrace you.'

That was when she turned towards me again, burning. 'Then perhaps you know something of him which I do not?'

Her eyes were on me, her attention concentrated. But observing something of my own perplexity, she appeared to soften once more. 'Forgive me. I make apology for my impatience. You, of all his companions, are the most consistent in his education upon necessity.' She seemed to breathe more slowly. 'Yet how is it that you do not irk him with your own constant reminders?'

'He turns me to his account, madam,' I said. 'He says if his childlessness is to be the source of such fine, high-minded verse, why then, he shall be obliged to honour it by living his life as it is.'

She smiled at that, despite herself, and said, 'He has a courtier's tongue, too, amongst his other attributes.'

'That, too,' I said.

'Which very attribute he could be employing to woo a bride.'

'He is hardly yet twenty, madam.'

She considered me a little slyly, still searching, I suspected, for advantage.

'And you, sir? In years, you are ... ?'

'Twenty-nine, madam.'

'Have you no offspring?'

'Three.'

'Ah, three.' She considered this new knowledge. 'And – forgive my enquiry, sir – what age were you when you fathered your firstborn?'

My mind drifted backwards. 'When I was seventeen or eighteen, madam. But surely – '

'And at your last child?' she insisted.

'Some twenty years of age, I believe. Yet I do not see – '

'Do you not, sir? My son is already as old as you were at your third child. I have no other children, and he has a duty upon his house.'

Perhaps because I sensed only too well her noble

obsession with the extension of her line, I felt powerless in the face of such a will. There were shadows of her own life, too, which I had no inclination to disturb. And so I attempted to maintain my expression, remaining equivocal, saying merely, 'I am your ally, madam.'

She raised her hand for me to kiss, and said, 'I have other matters to attend.'

'Then I shall depart,' I replied. 'And I thank you for your audience.'

Out of respect, I moved backwards towards the door. When I turned to depart, she had seated herself at her desk and was already concentrating on her correspondence.

I closed the door softly.

That night I sat at my own hard board, the flickering light of the little flame on the white face of the paper, writing feverishly. Through the open window I could see the moon shining on a dew-laden field. But I was oblivious of my surroundings. Occasionally I had recourse to a cup of wine. Sometimes, if my thoughts flowed well, or I found some hidden virtue in a phrase, I smiled to myself, nodded, dipped my quill in inky darkness, and began again to scratch the paper.

> *Look in thy glass and tell the face thou viewest*
> *Now is the time that face should form another;*
> *Whose fresh repair if now thou not renewest,*
> *Thou dost beguile the world, unbless some mother.*
> *For where is she so fair whose unear'd womb*
> *Disdains the tillage of thy husbandry?*
> *Or who is he so fond will be the tomb*
> *Of his self-love to stop posterity?*

A few days later I was walking with the Countess, side by side, along the great flagstones of one of the interior passages. She was reading aloud, apparently absorbed, as she continued the sonnet to its conclusion.

'Thou art thy mother's glass and she in thee
Calls back the lovely April of her prime:
So thou through windows of thine age shall see,
Despite of wrinkles, this thy golden time.'

She paused before enunciating the last two lines:

'But if thou live, remember'd not to be,
Die single and thine image dies with thee.'

She halted, lowered the page, turned and smiled at me.

'Who could resist such measured and unswerving advice?'

'Your son, madam,' I said. 'Only he.'

'And he is the only one who should heed it.'

'That is the world's way.'

'Then what is it holds him back?'

'The rites of spring, perhaps.'

'But we approach winter once more.'

In our walk along the corridor, we were passing by a window that overlooked the main courtyard. My attention was distracted for a moment by a movement outside.

'What holds you?' the Countess inquired.

Out of politeness, I halted so that she, turning around me, might have a better view. Following the direction of my gaze, she looked out through the same window, onto the courtyard, where a small retinue was moving across the cobbles.

At its head was a heavy old man, sitting on a great piebald horse. Several other riders followed at a respectful distance. Amongst them was a dark-haired, younger woman.

Following my gaze to the head of the column, my lady said, 'My Lord Hunsdon, the Lord Chamberlain. He visits us for several days.'

I nodded. At the same time, I could not help but continue to stare out, transfixed. Perhaps my lady noticed this unswerving attention, for she looked out at the little train again.

'Who is the lady, madam?' I asked.

'Why, Master Shakespeare, I believe you are smitten.'

Sensing her amusement, I replied, 'You forbid my further interest?'

'An Italian whore,' she said, 'since you ask.'

I added, as lightly as I could, 'Handsome, even so.'

'Handsome indeed,' she said, looking out again on the scene unfolding in the courtyard. 'She is fathered, as I remember, by one of the Queen's musicians, and has come to be his lordship's mistress. For colour, his lordship married her to a minstrel, so that he may continue to have her as he wishes – respectably.'

'The minstrel to whom she is married?' I asked. 'He rides beside her?'

'The young man? I believe so.'

'He seems even younger than she.'

'A mere stripling, as you say. But that is his purpose. The greener to his role. Meanwhile, the old boar will visit his sow as he wishes.'

Under the circumstances, perhaps, it was as much information as I could expect. My mind was already attempting to absorb the implications. With some reluctance I removed my attention from the sight of the procession, and so found myself facing her ladyship again. Her eyes were like lights. She seemed both agitated and amused by my interest.

I said, 'My Lord Hunsdon has his own players, for whom I have acted and penned the occasional entertainment.'

'Indeed. And so you have a proper interest in him, not merely in his whore.'

'I have an interest in many things, madam.'

The Countess smiled. 'And so you do, sir.' Her voice, which until now had been almost flirtatious, became commanding. 'Meanwhile, be so good as to maintain your interest in my son's duty. Now, I must attend to my own.'

Without waiting for my bow, she moved on. I observed her depart down the passage. As soon as she had disappeared, I felt it safe to return my attention once more to the procession.

In the courtyard, the dark lady dismounted. She was statuesque, with raven hair and a complexion that suggested something of her Italian ancestry. She looked round the courtyard imperiously. Nervously, the young man, her husband, approached and seemed to speak with her. But she hardly appeared to notice him, treating him almost as she would a servant.

Chapter 12

*I*T HAPPENED THAT I STRONGLY DESIRED to speak with my Lord Hunsdon, my former theatre patron, that venerable soldier and cousin of our Queen. For the next few days I attempted to engineer a meeting. But, howsoever I approached him, he seemed engaged in discussion with one or another of the visitors who seemed to throng the house. Two days later I saw him in the rose garden, strutting broad-shouldered like a raven in an empty field. His hands were on his hips, while he walked restlessly backwards and forwards, seeming deep in thought.

For several moments I considered, then stepped out

firmly towards him. As I approached, my Lord Hunsdon continued to pace. When I was nearly upon him, he raised his attention. An emotion touched his venerable face, briefly, like a fly on the face of a bull. Then, almost immediately, he resumed his walking. It was as though he were lost in a dream of contemplation, unwilling to be distracted from his thoughts. So I continued to walk past him without stopping.

It was only when I was about to leave the rose-garden that my Lord Hunsdon, as though waking from his reverie, called out, 'Master Shakespeare!' I halted and turned. He beckoned me back imperiously. As I approached, he said, 'Come, sir. You cannot avoid me so easily. I see everything, y'know. And what I do not see is not worth consideration.'

I made a brief bow. 'Your all-seeing lordship.'

'And tell me now,' he said, 'what mischief do you practise while the London theatres are closed?'

'I write verses, my lord, and work on a play.'

'Southampton keeps you?' he asked slyly.

'Most ably,' I replied.

'Now,' he said, drawing closer, 'now listen, damn you. I heard of a play you wrote, a most excellent play, that was recommended by a woman acquaintance.'

Speaking thus, he waved his arm towards a recessed part of the garden, where the same dark-haired woman I had previously observed now sat at a little distance in an arbour in the fleeting sunshine.

Following my gaze, my Lord Hunsdon said, 'One of my minstrels, Miss Bassano, now married to another, Master Lanier. You have met the young couple?'

'No, my lord.'

'Well, never mind, sir. She has read an actor's copy of your work and speaks most highly of it. Now, if I remember the title of it, let me see, now, the title of it, the name of it tips my tongue, it tips my tongue. Ah yes, dammit, yes, dammit, it comes now: *The Taming of the Shrew*.'

I nodded, saying, 'Written recently, perhaps a year ago.'

'And why did you not bring it me? Why not?'

'I waited my opportunity to speak to you in person.'

'Yet we speak now, and it is I who mention it you, courtesy of a lady.'

'You are most kind.'

'All-seeing, sir. All-seeing – though I am almost

blind in one eye. Have you seen the younger Walsingham?'

'No, my lord.'

His bold eyes considered me. 'That damn fox. He's
here. I'm damned if I've seen him, though. Slinking
through the brush. No sooner sighted than departed.'

While he talked so animatedly of Walsingham, I
looked over at the arbour, where it seemed Mrs Lanier
was quietly observing us. Meanwhile my Lord Hunsdon
continued, 'When you are in London, bring a copy of it
to me, do you hear? When the theatres open, it will be
our first performance. Damn me, *The Taming of the
Shrew*. There's a saucy title for you. Damn me.'

'Thank you, my lord. But I see you were preoccupied before I came. And therefore, with your kind permission, I will absent myself, and will leave you to your
thoughts.'

'Yes, yes ... If you see a fox, pray, report him to me.'

'At the first sight,' I said.

'And we will set our hounds after him.'

'He shall not brush us off, my lord.'

A smile spread on his old face. 'Heh, heh, damned

fine. Be off with you, you punning vagabond. And bring that play to me.'

He nodded once, out of courtesy, then began to walk up and down again. And so I knew that I was dismissed, and could return to my life again. I bowed to him. But before departing, I allowed myself one last glance at Emilia Lanier, seated calmly in the arbour.

Chapter 13

*E*ACH DAY FOLLOWED ANOTHER. One morning I was walking along one of the passages of the great house, inclining my head occasionally to people who passed, thinking to myself; how shall a man be smitten by a woman who is called behind her back a whore, who is Lord Hunsdon's mistress, who has been a paramour of several others of the great, all before she has reached the age of twenty-three?

During these ruminations I greeted several other people, embracing certain retainers from other great houses – scholars, tutors, secretaries, scribes, members of the scratching professions – and various others with whom I had in common an itch to exchange gossip. I had found, though I was in a provincial court, that there was a constant ebb and flow of guests to and from this great house. For while London was in plague the court itself was dispersed, as much as we poor players. And so one might find, in the antechambers and halls, great men conspiring in little corners. There was one in particular for whom I kept an eye upon, for reasons of my own.

It happened that one day a group of several men passed me in a corridor. I recognised red hair, almost albino eyes, and bowed more deeply to one in particular than to the others.

'Sir Thomas,' I said, raising my head. Sir Thomas Walsingham was a cold, interior man, younger kinsman of Sir Francis, the Queen's great spymaster, who had died several years before. He had inherited the family reputation for intrigue. Now he turned slowly, as though he recognised me. This compelled me to turn with him, so that we were like two objects circling one another, earth and moon.

'Why, Master Shakespeare,' he said.

The three stalwarts who accompanied him until

then had stood back while we conducted our manoeuvre. As we came to rest, so they, like other moons, lined up behind the curve of his shoulder. It did not pass my notice that all three were muscular and heavy, that each had the build of a torturer.

Walsingham opened his account, in his usual manner, saying, 'I have a riddle for you, sir, which I would dearly have you answer. What bird is it that singeth most sweetly for his supper?'

'A poet, I believe.'

Behind him his retainers stirred a little. He turned to his companions with a mocking, portentous movement, saying, 'A bird of wit.'

'You employ greater wits than I,' I said.

'Master Marlowe?' he enquired. 'Indeed, but Master Marlowe hath a complex tongue. And sometimes, he being so witty, we his companions do not entirely know what he sings.'

The other men smiled at this allusion.

We were in a place that was open to observation by others, and so he pointed to a recess which lay out of sight of the main passage. In a single body, we moved there, I perhaps a little uncomfortably, but carried by the general will. Out of sight of the passing traffic, Walsingham turned to me again and spoke *sotto voce*.

'I look upon you for a favour, sir.'

'A favour?' I asked, surprised.

'Indeed, I would request that you deliver a message.'

At the same moment he indicated one of his henchmen who, from the depths of his clothes, produced a sealed letter and held it out to me. Without touching it, I read the name of the person to whom it was addressed.

Walsingham said, 'A simple letter, intended for my Lord Southampton.'

I was now alarmed. To hide my consternation, and to gather a few precious seconds, I said, 'I feel certain, sir, that if it is from you, he should receive it from you directly.'

'Unlike you, sir, I do not make his acquaintance every day.'

It seemed to me there was an element of insinuation in what he said. The silence floated between us.

'Even so,' I smiled to allay as best I could. 'I do believe it would better come from you.'

Walsingham's expression became colder. He said, 'Your scribbling, now. It keeps you and your young family?'

'We survive, sir.'

'Indeed,' he said, 'you survive.'

He gestured to another of his henchmen, who produced from one of his deep sleeves a small purse. 'Then perhaps we may add to your good fortune. Twenty gold florins for a small mission, nothing more. A letter, sir, to a patron you would see in normal course.'

'I am grateful for your interest,' I said. 'But I deduce that, for twenty florins, the message must be one of importance. And since, therefore, I am not of importance myself, but a simple scribbler, why, I assume that twenty florins and I shall not be suited.'

The atmosphere between us, which had been cold, now grew colder still. The letter and the bag of florins continued to be held out towards me, like temptations. For what seemed to be an unconscionable time, four pairs of cold eyes regarded me. Then Walsingham nodded to his henchmen again, and both offerings were summarily withdrawn.

Now my tempter said, 'I perceive that you and Mr

Marlowe, whom you hold so highly, must be different men.'

'That may be so, sir.'

'Master Marlowe hath strong opinions, and involves himself in the movements of the day.'

'He is a greater man than I,' I said.

'My compliments to my Lord Southampton, on choosing trustworthy friends.'

Delivered coldly, this seemed more criticism than compliment. After that, he turned his back to me and departed, his henchmen following him like faithful dogs.

I observed him grow smaller, and felt a shadow had passed across my life, like a wave that washes back from striking a sea wall, subverting other waves. With it came the terrible intuition that if I had accepted the bribe once, I would forever be in the society of conspirators and torturers.

Chapter 14

THOUGH I ATTENDED upon my Lord Southampton during the day, and bent to my poor verses at night, throughout that winter I hunted for one presence. My Lord Hunsdon visited several times, accompanied by his retinue. So it was that one morning I was walking across a courtyard, engaged in my own thoughts, when I heard, through a window, the virginals being played. The keys were being struck with such thoughtful precision and dexterity that I halted, like an animal enchanted, and leaned against the wall, listening to the beautiful notes.

Following the sound, I made a detour from my

intended course, and entered the building through a side door. It was not a part of the great house that I normally visited – an old granary or chapter, used for dancing lessons, or the practising of music. At first I found myself in a passage, hearing the faint notes of the virginals as though still a little way off.

I followed the notes, like a man following a scent. Eventually I arrived at a place where the sound was loudest. Raising my hand, I pressed on the door; a room like a small hall opened before me.

At the end of the room, Emilia Lanier was seated at the keys. She paused when I entered, turning towards me slowly.

'Play on, madam,' I said, remembering a line on which I had been working, feeling for the scansion in some recess of my memory. 'If love be the food of music,' I said, 'play on.' That didn't sound quite right. I resolved to work upon it.

She looked at me, then turned back to the instrument and with her light fingers perpetuated the air.

While the notes sang, I walked into the room, sat down on a bench a few feet away from her upright back, leaning against a neighbouring wall. Closing my eyes I entered that state of contemplation which is the province of devout monks and lovers. And there I remained, for how long I do not remember, lost from grace until Emilia Lanier finished her tune, turned towards me, and smiled.

I said, 'I believe I owe you my gratitude.'

'For what, sir?' she asked.

'For speaking to my Lord Hunsdon favourably, about a play of mine – *The Taming of the Shrew*.'

'It is a fine play,' she said, 'on the outside very crude and fierce; and on the inside ... subtle.'

'My Lord Hunsdon is now here in this house again?' I asked. 'I have not seen him.'

'He has departed on a journey to a military outpost which he says is too cold and bitter for my temperament. He leaves me here to wait his return.'

I smiled. 'In honour of your temperament, madam, which, by contrast, is warm, and sunny, and perhaps inclined to generosity.'

'Towards those whom it admires.'

So we continued, bantering happily. And so it struck me, not for the first time, that in each profession there is a nobility; even in harlotry. Though I might be the companion and mentor of a great lord, and think myself a gentleman, yet there was something between us that was like music. She brought my plays to Lord Hunsdon's attention. She carried a certain beauty of thought to that gruff old soldier, that Warden of the East Marches. And she played the virginals with such sympathy of feeling that sometimes I thought that we were performers both, and that in our lives our only purpose was that we should play our roles as best we might.

We continued through the morning, she playing and I listening, talking alternately, as though old friends. When she finished playing and stood up, I followed her example and we two faced each other. Emilia held out her hand towards me with a graceful, formal precision. Carefully, I took her hand in mine. She did not resist, but at the same time she said gently, 'My Lord Hunsdon is your former patron. And he would be your patron again.'

'Indeed, madam,' I said, 'and it is you who put him in mind of me, for which I am eternally grateful.' I leaned forward and kissed her hand, but she said softly, 'I do not ask for recompense.'

I raised my eyes to meet hers. 'Recompense is deserved, madam, even if not asked for.'

She considered me with amusement. 'You would do well to listen to what I say.'

'I listen to your music, madam,' I said, 'And my heart answers.'

Emilia continued to regard me. Then she pulled her hand – still gripped in my own – gently but firmly away from me. Having disentangled herself, she placed her own two palms around my left hand, and drew it gently towards her face. It seemed she was about to kiss my hand. A thrill passed through me, for she seemed to be signalling that she returned my desire. I observed her progress. As she brought my left hand to her lips, I watched in fascination. She opened her mouth, her lips touched my hand, and then I felt a searing pain as she bit into me savagely.

I heard my own cry of agony and pulled my hand away, staggering backwards to the neighbouring wall. There I crouched over my wound, nursing my bleeding hand with my other. I brought it to my mouth to lick away the blood, meanwhile watching her observe me almost considerately.

I began to protest. 'Madam ... '

But she, by contrast, seemed to have returned to her original composure. Now she calmly said, 'I warned you to listen to what I say.'

'It seems I did not hear,' I said.

'Then listen to me now. Do not bite the hand that feeds you.'

With my free hand, I reached into my sleeve for a kerchief and began to wind it around my bleeding paw. Using my teeth and free hand, I attempted to tie a knot. Between these attempts to bind my wound, I conducted a brief conversation with her, beginning, 'You are loyal to your master.'

'No, I am loyal to you. You should not mortgage your destiny to a merely furtive pleasure.'

'A merely furtive pleasure! As you are his mistress, madam, I believe I will stand being lectured by you on furtive pleasures.'

'My Lord Hunsdon has married me to a young man in his employ. I am become respectable.'

'Becoming is not being,' I said.

'Do not be bitter,' she said.

'Bitten, more likely, madam.'

'I bit your left hand,' she said, 'so that you may continue to write with your right.'

'How kind you are, madam,' I rejoined, 'Praise be I am not sinister.'

The initial pain and shock of her bite had partially subsided. I had more or less succeeded in tying my kerchief with a knot. I even began to see some small vestige of humour in my situation. Holding up my bound hand, I said, 'Truly, madam, my Lord Hunsdon hath no need of a hound to protect him, if he has you.'

'I protect you, sir, as well as him.'

'Then you bite your own master.'

'I will continue to protect you – against your will, if necessary.'

Raising my bound hand, I said, 'And I will continue to wear this as a keepsake. Now,' – I made a mock furtive glance towards the door, as though planning my escape, and with an actor's relish I began to sidle sideways along the wall, towards the door, saying – 'if you will be kind enough to allow me an avenue of safe passage, I hope that you will not consider protecting me again.'

She watched my antics with hardly suppressed

amusement, even raising a hand to her mouth to hide a smile.

I reacted to her gesture with mock fright. 'Careful, madam ... '

By then I had reached the door. Still with my back to it, I carefully edged through the opening, and exited stage right, slamming the door closed behind me in comical relief.

Inside the room I heard her burst into loud laughter. Then she must have paused briefly, because silence ensued. But mirth must have overtaken her once more, because she burst into loud laughter again.

I do not know what further changes took place inside the blessed music room, how many swift changes of mood may have passed, except that another period of silence followed. I moved down the passageway, towards the outside of the building.

Perhaps she sat down at the virginals. Perhaps she considered the keys for a while. By the time I was outside, passing by the window, I heard her begin playing again, though this time the tune was 'Greensleeves', that popular and sentimental lament.

Can one play music with irony? I do not know. But I believe I heard it then – something of bitterness and amusement imparted through those fingers. It seemed to me that just as I had overacted my departure for her amusement, so now the melodious strains signalled a response – as though she too, for my own entertainment, mocked her own sadness.

Her music followed me as I made my way across the quadrangle. I paused for a moment, looked down at my wounded hand, glanced once more at the open window, hoping, perhaps, to see her again, then shook my head and walked on.

Chapter 15

*T*HAT NIGHT I ATTEMPTED TO WRITE, but could not. I sat with my quill in my right hand, my wounded left hand resting on the table, staring forward into the darkness. It was not the pain itself but the shock of her admonishment. What she had done burned me too deep and close for objective consideration. Instead I sat at my board and, after a certain time, unable either to compose or to dissemble, I fell asleep upon my duty.

I lay there until light began to pour in through the small window. In luminous dawn, my hand burned still. Before my lord's household stirred, I took it upon myself to leave my room and walk down to the small stream that passed the main house a hundred paces away. There I bathed my wound, and put on a fresh covering of cloth. But I was still in agitation. It seemed to me that any truth which is inflicted from the outside is like a poison to the unwilling. I resolved to find her when I could and make my apologies, the interval having granted me at least the beginnings of sincerity.

When I had bathed and dressed my hand I walked to the rose garden, where early mists lingered. There my restlessness continued. I must have walked up and down for the best part of an hour, preoccupied, moving back and forth, my wounded hand clasped by the other behind my back. I was so absorbed I did not hear the sound of a retinue approaching, the faint tinkle and fret of a harness, until I was hailed directly by a half-familiar voice. 'Master Shakespeare!'

I turned round. My Lord Hunsdon was seated on his heavy piebald horse, with several mounted retainers halted behind him. When I had gathered my senses I recalled that he had a reputation for travelling by night. It was said that since no one else travelled the roads during the dark hours, he would not be noticed as he went about his duties of inspection. It was also reported that he liked nothing more than to appear at some outpost or stronghold in dawn's early mist, before anyone was much awake, in order to catch sentries unawares and make his private assessments. If so, it seemed to have become a habit of his old age. Now he had surprised me, with my hand still bandaged from his mistress's attentions.

In dawn's early mist I observed him slowly dismount and walk towards me with his old horseman's barrel roll. 'You seem preoccupied, Master Shakespeare.'

I nodded in greeting and distant agreement.

Halting in front of me, he took hold of my bandaged hand, firmly but gently, and raised it to his closer view. 'Why, I believe you are wounded.'

I inclined my head again.

'I am a soldier, sir, and expert upon such matters.' He raised his wise old eyes to mine. 'The cause, tell me now, the cause?'

'A hound, my lord.'

'A hound? He should be whipped.'

'A faithful female hound,' I said. 'Who merely did her duty.'

My Lord Hunsdon's eyes stared calmly into my own. Their expression reminded me of the eyes of a pike when one looks over a riverbank, and sees – firm and unflinching – yellow eyes regarding you. At the same time, I detected a faint and somewhat steely glimmer of amusement in his expression.

'Beware of female teeth,' he said at last.

'Indeed, my lord.'

'Behind them there are strong emotions.'

While he talked, he was busily engaged in undoing the bandage. The wound was exposed.

'It no longer bleeds,' he said.

'Then I believe I am forgiven,' I replied.

His pike's eyes, rising again, looked into mine. 'This hound ... forgives you?' He paused a second time for his own calm consideration and amusement. 'Good. Forgiveness purifies. Give it air, sir, is my advice.'

'I will, my lord.'

It seemed he had extracted as much entertainment as he desired from my condition. Now he lowered his voice. 'I return to collect my mistress, and to pay my respects to our Countess.'

I said nothing, grateful above all that he had seen

fit to change the subject. He continued, 'You shall visit me in London, when the theatres open.'

'Thank you, my lord.'

The glint of amusement hovered in his expression. He leant towards me again, and whispered in his throaty voice, with what seemed to me a certain degree of theatrical relish, 'And keep away from faithful female hounds.'

Then he nodded, turned, remounted his horse, and at the head of the retinue rode into the main court of the house. I watched him depart.

Of what strange components is loyalty compounded? My own disloyalty had been noticed, calmly exposed and, it seemed, jovially and liberally forgiven, with no more than a soldier's considered warning. And what was perhaps strangest of all was that in the very act of forgiveness my old patron had reclaimed my lifelong adherence to him, to his causes and his heirs.

Chapter 16

*U*NTIL THEN I HAD FELT UNABLE TO WRITE. It was not merely the literal pain of Emilia's bite, but rather that she had forbidden my love in the name of my art – as though I myself were not sufficient curator of my own meagre talent. Since my Lord Hunsdon had also forgiven me, I felt moved to compose a private valediction of our love, if only because sometimes the expression of a feeling acts to relieve the writer of some more morbid anguish. As I have found in the past, intense emotion sometimes drives the pen with a certain lucid force. After a period of concentration, I managed to write:

If I hear music in the painted day,
Drawing myself towards those fateful sounds,
And all my thoughts move outward to the lay,
Like lines of scent on which run faithful hounds,
Then I must hide my thoughts in careful praise
Which, praising you, fall short of what I feel.
If I should moan your loss, make better days
The sad account of my most bitter meal:
Your fingers on the cloth, touching their hem,
Press me to sit and watch your subtle hands;
The singular white thoughts which rise from them,
Graceful as hinds towards that hidden land.
    O, let me sit beside you while you play,
    Allowing thoughts to alter night for day.

When I had finished the poem, I read it through several times to check the beat and rhythm. The piece was flawed in certain places, and needed further work, but at least it expressed the glimmer of something that I felt. I was satisfied that I had caught my sense of anguish, although briefly and imperfectly. In that respect, it had served its cathartic purpose. Raising the page, I held it to the candle flame and watched as that soft and savage form lovingly devoured it. So, it seemed to me, I cleaned my mind of my forbidden love, though in truth I could not persuade myself that some ashes did not remain.

Chapter 17

OVER THE NEXT FEW DAYS I felt a sense of exalta-
tion, knowing that any danger of reprisal from my Lord
Hunsdon had passed. Now I looked about me at the
cold winter countryside beyond the walls of the garden,
the shadows of the great bare oaks which overhung the
meadows.

Something still agitated me. I was about to sink
into my thoughts, return to my pacing, when I heard a
faint tune, a scent of music, from the virginals.

Glancing around, I listened, then began to walk
towards the sound. It came through the same window,
from the same room in which Emilia last played.

Perhaps a benign fate was granting me one final opportunity to make apologies before she departed with her master.

So I hurried towards the room, entering by the usual side entrance. Travelling along the passage, I paused at the door, and opened it.

A dark-haired young woman was playing at the keys, but it was not Emilia. She halted at my sudden entrance, turning her head towards me.

I said, 'Madam Florio.'

'Clearly, sir, from your expression I see that you did not expect me.'

'I apologise for interrupting you. I expected ... another.'

'Emilia?' she smiled.

'Perhaps.'

'How strange. She asked me to play this morning, though she did not say for what purpose. As she is my friend, I could think of no good reason for not granting her wish.'

'I believe she is about to depart.'

'Why, yes, Lord Hunsdon has returned for her.'

Out of the window I could see, in the main court-yard, Emilia on my Lord Hunsdon's arm, and the train of baggage horses being assembled behind them. I observed beauty beside her wise, old beast.

To Lucia, I said, 'Madam, may I ... listen?'

Lucia smiled. 'Of course.'

I sat down on the nearby bench, though somewhat thoughtfully.

She, as one who was constantly ministering to others of her family, had little time to feed herself, and had set a half-eaten apple down beside on the side of the instrument. She hesitated again before striking the keys. To encourage her, I said, 'If food be the music of love, play on.' No, that didn't seem quite right, either.

Lucia smiled at me. She paused, a little self-consciously, in front of the keys, then began to play. At first her notes seemed to falter. She halted, turned to look at me. I nodded and smiled further encouragement. She returned to the keyboard, composed herself, inclined her head once in rhythm, and commenced again.

Now she seemed to pick the theme. Her fingers

started to skip, she began to play with lightness and elegance. I watched her fingers nimbly moving over the keys.

In my room that night, I wrote:

How oft when thou, my music, music play'st,
Upon that blessed wood whose motion sounds
With thy sweet fingers, when thou gently sway'st
The wiry concord that mine ear confounds,
Do I envy those jacks that nimble leap
To kiss the tender inward of thy hand,
    Whilst my poor lips, which should that harvest reap,
    At the wood's boldness by thee blushing stand!

In my Lord Southampton's rooms that evening, my host sat in his chair by a great fire, reading aloud, taking up the theme:

To be so tickl'd, they would change their state
And situation with those dancing chips,
O'er whom thy fingers walk with gentle gait,
Making dead wood more bless'd than living lips.

Since saucy jacks so happy are in this,
Give them thy fingers, me thy lips to kiss.

My lord paused for a moment, then raised his attention from the page. '"*Since saucy jacks* ... " John Florio, her husband, my tutor, is a "jack", is he not? And if he is happy with her fingers, why, you may be happy with her lips.' He smiled at his analysis. 'A most rich and lewd conceit.'

But now, as other matters impressed, his expression sobered and then seemed to darken. He rose from his chair and paced up and down, saying, after several moments, 'I also have something for you to read.'

He walked over to a pile of documents upon his writing desk, picked up one, raised it, identified it with a brief examination, and handed it to me, accompanied by the words, 'Consider it carefully.'

For several moments I studied the stern and dominating hand – the hand of a scholar – disciplined, upright, rigorous. It was written with a brisk economy in which I recognised the authentic style of Master Florio.

My lord, meanwhile, continued to pace and discourse. 'I told you that damned spy was writing his reports of me. I became intrigued to find out how he magicked his messages to his master. Several days ago, I observed him ride out from this house, as though taking the air. I registered carefully the direction in which he departed and, after a suitable interval, rode after him. He crossed the stream and entered the woods, then proceeded perhaps a furlong into their fastness. Out of caution, I dismounted and walked my horse. In a clearing I observed him meet three other horsemen, and pass what seemed a document to them. While they talked amongst themselves, I retreated into hiding. When the three horseman had conducted their business with Master Florio, they returned by the way they had come. I took another path, which I calculated would take me to a place ahead of them on their journey. And there I waited for them.'

As he talked, I envisaged the scene.

Chapter 18

MY LORD SAT ON HIS HORSE, in the little valley, his chosen defile, facing down the empty track, steep slopes on either side. Ahead of him, hidden by a tongue of woodland, a horse neighed. Then three riders turned the corner. They were covered in dark cloaks and hoods.

The waiting youth, controlling his restless stallion, considered them as they rode towards him. There was something calm and forbidding about him, this warrior's son – not least in the manner his horse quartered back and forth, dominating the pathway – which caused the three horsemen to pause on the path in front of him. There they halted.

It seemed to the solitary rider that the horseman in the middle of the three was the leader of that troupe. Heavy, broad-shouldered, his powerful war-horse took several steps forward, while his companions hung back as though in deference. In an authoritative voice he called out, 'I request that you stand aside, sir.'

The young earl did not move. Instead he said coldly, 'Announce yourself, and name your companions.'

There was a moment's pause between the confronting parties, as though the three horsemen were deciding whether to risk riding past their questioner. Then their leader sang out again, deep and cold, 'We are Lord Burghley's men, on the business of the Privy Council.'

'Show your livery,' demanded our solitary rider.

'Who asks?' demanded their leader.

'Henry Wriothesley, Earl of Southampton.'

The three horsemen whispered a few words among themselves. Then something else passed between them, something lighter, a note of sly mirth. It seemed that the single rider was transformed from a warrior into a nubile youth, swimming in a lake. One of the three horsemen was heard to say, 'Ask him to quote you a pretty verse.' Another said, 'Perhaps he will swim naked for us.' More laughter passed between them, moving backwards and forwards like a ripple of water, while the single rider watched them dispassionately.

Then the leader, asserting his status once again, unfastened his riding cloak, showing Lord Burghley's vertical green and black striped livery. Observing this, Southampton said, 'I must warn you that you trespass my estates.'

'This is a lawful common path.'

'That may be so. But you have upon your persons a document which is rightfully mine. And therefore – one such thing following another – I must proclaim you common thieves.'

There was another ripple of laughter between the three. At the same time, perhaps because animals have superior senses, a certain restlessness seemed to spread among their horses. Their leader said, 'We have no such document, except what is lawful.'

My lord said casually, as though stating a point of law, 'I have given you my warning.'

There was another brief animation of restless horses. Then the leader of the three said, 'And we have received it.' Placing his hand on his sword-hilt, he said, 'Now stand aside.'

But, despite the proclamation, the young earl stood his ground, observing his opponents calmly, announcing as though across the breakfast table, 'It seems enough has now been said between us, all diplomacy exhausted.'

So saying, he spurred his horse forward. The stallion pranced merrily, dauntless and bold. At first it seemed as if he were going to ride past his opponents and return to his house. But as he drew abreast the left-hand side of the three horsemen, he reached out casually, as though in greeting, or to tap a shoulder, except that his fingers lightly spread around the nearest horseman's chin and neck. At the same time, the young earl's fingers gripped like talons, he spurred his own mount forward, hauling his armed opponent backward off his horse, so that he fell heavily into the dust of the common path.

There followed an *affray*, or what the French sometimes call a *mêlée*, of plunging and screaming horses. The two remaining horsemen were still too close to each other to lay about them with their swords. In the confusion, my Lord Southampton's fist, in its heavy riding glove, struck the side of the face of a second rider, who also tumbled into the dust.

The two remaining riders circled each other, though the earl was without armament. His armed opponent, at last with sufficient space to use his sword arm, swung his weapon backwards, ready to strike, and manoeuvred to come alongside. But if one horseman was ready to strike, the other was armed with cunning. As the swordsman attempted to come within striking distance, so the earl swung his stallion to face the other, always keeping his own body a sword's length from disaster, while the two stallions pranced like rivals in love, baring teeth, angry as their riders. At the same time as the earl held himself distant from sword-strike, he urged his horse forwards, driving the other horse backwards towards a grove of oak trees at the side of the defile.

For a time the two stallions screamed and bit and reared in that small valley, the earl manoeuvring the other horse constantly backwards, deliberately cutting and driving, until the leader's horse struck a tree trunk, crushing the rider's leg, causing him to cry out in anguish, and in turn causing his frightened horse to rear and throw him off.

The horseman regained his feet and backed away, limping, towards a nearby grove of trees. My lord dismounted from his horse and followed him. The leader retreated until his back touched the trunk of one of the trees, as though for security.

There the two faced each other. But if the earl intended to speak, the other man now pre-empted him. 'My Lord Southampton, I give you fair warning that any man who touches a person in the livery of Lord Burghley, strikes at the authority of the Privy Council.'

My lord held out his hand, opened his palm, saying, 'The document.'

At this demand, the jaw of the leader hardened. 'I acknowledge no property of yours.'

My lord reached his hand into the other's clothes, deftly hauling out the sealed document hidden in his livery. He raised the paper to the other's eyes, saying, 'You do not acknowledge this?'

'That letter is sealed and is addressed to my Lord Burghley.'

'Why then, if he spies on me, I shall return the compliment. I hereby confiscate this article.'

White-faced, defiant, the horseman said, 'I will report your action to my master.'

My lord stowed the document in his own clothes. He removed one of his heavy riding gloves. Holding the glove in his right hand, he said, 'What you will report to your master is also this.' Then he struck his opponent so hard across his face with the glove, his head was forced sideways.

Under the sunlight in the clearing, there was an intake of breath as the leader absorbed the full weight of the insult. He was motionless at first, then slowly returned his white face and burning eyes to face his tormentor. Face to face, my lord seized the other's right hand with his left, placed the glove in its palm and said, 'Take this to your master, and speak thus: "If you wish to take issue with me, then do so to my face, and not behind my back, like a common thief."'

The leader could do nothing but observe as his assailant turned and walked back to his horse, mounted, swung his leg astride, and rode away.

Chapter 19

IN HIS ROOMS THAT NIGHT, I observed my host walking up and down. Anger made him light. He paused to say, 'I believe Lord Burghley will receive my message before another day is out.'

He interrupted his pacing to turn towards me so that he could judge my response. 'How do you answer?' he said.

'My lord,' I began, unsure how to proceed, 'I do not know the consequences.'

'My dear Master William, I do not pretend to know the consequences either – except this, that I have challenged my great, cold guardian to show his open hand.'

'You think he will answer your challenge?'

'I am certain of it. But he will answer in his own time, and in his own manner. I am no longer a child, to be intimidated. It is time to open my account with my Lord Burghley.' He pointed to the letter in my hand. 'But now, sir, we come to the missive itself, for which I risked my own safety. Perhaps you would be so kind as to remind me of its contents.'

I hesitated. He had begun pacing again. Now he observed my hesitation, stopped and made a brief ironic gesture for me to read out loud. So I cleared my throat and began:

To the Right Honourable William Cecil, Baron of Burghley
   My Most Esteemed Lordship –
   I write in mixed exasperation and anger to inform you that I can make no further impression upon our youthful charge who, despite my most earnest entreaties that he should conduct himself soberly and chastely, yet ignores my advice and good offices, and continues in his ways. He loses himself in masques and feasts, and carouses to excess. In addition, he keeps the lowest company, in the form of a cer-

tain actor and sometime writer of vulgar plays called William Shakespeare, who in turn fancies himself a poet. I most earnestly believe the said Shakespeare's influence is harmful upon our subject, being full of silly ditties of love, which distract our impressionable youth from his proper actions and considerations. In the course of my own duties as tutor, I have seen certain of these supposed sonnets in my Lord Southampton's chambers, and would have made a copy of some of them to act as evidence for your eyes, except that they are of such airy nonsense that I would not deem them suitable for your most esteemed consideration.

To keep a closer watch on this rhyme-maker, I offer him the use of my small library, so that at least while he pilfers my scholarship for his own purposes, he is not in the company of our young charge. Meanwhile, the account of my generosity is that the aforesaid rhymer plagues me with questions about Florence, and Genoa and Venice, and other such places, which he conceives as the settings of scenes or plays, for he has only the vaguest idea of geography in that region. Why, he thinks Milan a seaport and that Bohemia hath a coast!

I remain convinced that this magpie must be dismissed,

so that our charge may be brought to sobriety, towards
which end I will bend my intentions.

Meanwhile, Your Worshipful Lordship,

I remain, Yr. mst. humble servant,

Johannes Florio, Scholar

I finished reading. My ears burned at the various
charges of being a bumpkin, though in my circumstances I should have become used to the charges by
now. I was shaken out of my reverie, however, by my
patron, who had stopped stalking and was now considering me with a calm but fervent expression.

My lord said, 'A nimble jack indeed, whose hand is
truly turned against his own master.'

I could not find it in myself to disagree. 'It seems he
disappoints your trust.'

'Indeed,' he replied, gazing up at the ceiling,
announcing, in exasperation, and as though to a wider
audience, 'Master Florio disappoints our trust.'

Now he began to pace up and down again, attempting at the same time to withhold his rage. 'By all that
reasons, I should dismiss the traitor from my livery.'

While my patron raged and reflected, I thought not

so much of Florio himself, but of his wife and young family, turned out of employment and set upon the road. And so it happened that, despite the excess of insults that had been directed at me, I tempered my opinion.

'That would be justified, certainly,' I said. 'But would it be the wisest course?'

'Why would it not?' he asked.

'Is it not better to know the identity of Burghley's man, than not to know?'

'In what manner? His guilt has been established.'

'Knowing his identity, one may use him as a conduit, to convey whatever message one wishes to convey.'

My lord, who had been pacing rhythmically, halted now, though somewhat cautiously and reluctantly. 'Cleverly argued. But then I am baulked of my desire for honest retribution.'

'Revenge may be enjoyed in its own time.'

He observed me for several moments. 'So be it. Then let us turn our attention to other matters which interest us.'

'Which other matters, my lord?'

'Let us consider the subject of your poem.'

'Which subject in particular?'

'Madam Florio, playing upon the virginals.' He turned towards me. 'You find Master Florio's wife to your liking?'

Perhaps, in answering his question as fully as I did, I tried to deflect him from what I suspected he might now intend. I said, 'One of her brothers is the poet, Samuel Daniel. Her father is a music master, as is her other brother. She is now the wife of a great scholar. And she seems to have absorbed the best influences from each, for she writes verse, she plays music, and she has a scholarly application. Yes, she is to my liking.'

To which he replied, 'On all these points I am in agreement. Which, adding each to each, would make her seduction all the sweeter.'

'Seduction?'

'From Latin, *seducio*, *seducere*. As Master Florio would tell you. To lead to oneself.'

'You would seduce her?'

'Or you would.' He paused. 'One or another way, I will have my revenge on Master Florio.'

My lord returned once more to his angry pacing, locked in his own thoughts, while I observed him, my expression equivocal.

Chapter 20

THAT NIGHT I LAY ON MY BED, staring up at the ceiling, fretting, sleepless by turns, eyelids leaning against the night, my thoughts far distant.

The next morning I stood outside the door of the room which held the virginals, from which sweet music could be heard within.

Pausing there, I listened to the notes, then smoothly pushed my entrance, expecting what I saw, seeing what I expected – Lucia practising on the instrument, her fingers dancing over the jacks.

Becoming aware of me, she turned briefly, regarded

me, smiled trustingly, then pursued the shimmering and rapid movements of her hands.

I stood in the doorway, until she halted her playing and looked up, guileless, at her interloper, who now advanced towards her across the floor. His calculated footsteps, hollowing their tones, echoed his heart. Immodest, shameless, he sat down on the empty bench beside her.

She said, 'You see, sir, how you have encouraged me in my practice.'

'You need no encouragement, madam,' I said. 'If music be the food of love, play on.' The sentence scanned well, and sounded in tune, at least. Even so, my words seemed false.

Meanwhile she would insist, babbling on, sweetly disingenuous, 'I have had several children, and had forgot my musical studies. Now I find myself able to return. You see how it is.'

My expression was sympathetic, but perhaps distracted. So it was she who, noticing some silence at my core, said, 'Sir, it is you who seem preoccupied.'

I could not answer, lost in my own thoughts. It was her innocence that silenced me. When finally I raised my face, I knew I must give her some warning, some alert, and felt compelled to measure out the danger. So I began, 'I am obliged to forewarn you, madam.'

'Warn me?' she asked, curious at first, displaying no immediate alarm.

'Yes,' I confirmed.

'Of what?'

'Of a danger.'

'To whom?'

'To yourself.'

Her eyes opened wider. 'To me?'

'To you.'

'Of violence?'

'No, madam. A suit of passion. Aimed at you.'

'From whom?'

'From me.'

She was silent for several long moments, during which time I returned to my own thoughts.

I expected that she might begin to play. But suddenly, as though by swift election, Lucia was standing, looking down on me, her expression in sweet and deep turmoil. Almost before I knew it she had parted her knees, was seated astride my legs, facing me. She placed her hand round the back of my head, pulled my face to her neck, murmured softly and passionately, 'I knew it, oh, I knew it, from the way that you looked at me, I knew. Oh do not be ashamed, do not be ashamed ... '

I was about to object, but just as I raised my face from the warmth of her neck, she smothered my words with her lips.

My hands, which were about to push her away, stuttered, seemed to hesitate; then, of their own volition, they tightened around her waist and held her. Our embrace was fierce and urgent. She reached down with her hand, raised her dress, freed me from my cloth, positioned herself, rose up and down on me. Carried away, she seemed about to cry out, until my hand closed gently but firmly over her mouth.

I had heard a sound in the passageway outside, distinctive steps. We both turned, frightened as deer, while footsteps in the passage outside approached the door. They seemed to pause outside. After a while they passed.

Lucia let out a gasp, rising from me. She pulled her dress back into decency. I followed suit. Facing one another, both of us poised on the cusp of our passion, it was she who said, 'Do not be ashamed, I beg you.'

'I am sorry, madam, I took advantage of your kindness towards me – '

'No, no, no – ' she said.

But I insisted, 'Return to your playing, I beg you. I should not have compromised you by visiting you alone. I will depart now.'

Yet she seemed determined upon a final throw, 'No, you are wrong, women do not retreat in matters of love. I should have risked ... ' She breathed out, 'I should have risked everything.'

Struggling to control myself, I bowed and left. In the passage outside, I looked up and down, relieved at not being seen. I leaned against the door, breathing deeply for a few moments, before departing. Inside the room, I could envisage how sweet Lucia listened, eyes wide with passion, to my retreating footsteps. I imagined her returning to the virginals. Shy as leaves, I could imagine how her fingers touched the jacks. But she seemed in too much turmoil to play.

Chapter 21

THAT NIGHT I PUT MY FACE IN MY HANDS, in deepest thought and abject misery, recalling the episode in which I had been both actor and merciless observer. It was not the act itself, but my own motives, from which I recoiled most deeply. When I raised my face from my hands, I attempted to compose myself. I sat down at the bench. My board at least was a small consolation. I reached for my quill, dipped it in ink, paused, then began to write. After a time I halted, hesitated, looked at the first and second lines, crossed them out, began again, and so on, half a dozen times, until the black beginning took its shape, and the rest of the piece followed.

> The expense of spirit in a waste of shame
> Is lust in action; and till action, lust
> Is perjur'd, murderous, bloody, full of blame,
> Savage, extreme, rude, cruel, not to trust;
> Enjoy'd no sooner but despised straight,
> Past reason hunted, and no sooner had,
> Past reason hated, as a swallow'd bait,
> On purpose laid to make the taker mad:
> Mad in pursuit, and in possession so;
> Had, having, and in quest to have, extreme;
> A bliss in proof, – and prov'd, a very woe;
> Before, a joy propos'd; behind, a dream.
>   And this the world well knows; yet none knows well
>   To shun the heaven that leads men to this hell.

When I finished the poem, my vision became progressively darker, until it seemed the final lines blackened into deep night.

Chapter 22

MY LORD AND I were each in chairs seated close to a roaring fire. After his first reading of the verse, he flung down the written page, crying out, 'Damn this. Damn this. I feel I should apologise. Not only to you, but to her.'

I continued to stare into the fire. But he, as though seeking some displacement, agitated beyond measure, seized a strong brass poker and turned the logs energetically.

After a few seconds, I said, 'You are not to blame. It was I who took advantage of her.'

But he, contradicting my equivocation, said, 'No, not so. The blame is mine alone.'

'Even so – ' I began.

'Even so,' he said.

'Even so, my lord, the error being mine, perhaps we should no longer use an innocent woman to serve our purposes against Master Florio.'

He rose from his chair and began to stalk the room. After a while he paused. 'I am properly admonished. Let us, as you suggest, cease this deployment.'

But I said, 'It is not so easy, now.'

'Why not?' he turned, and I saw something there – some continuation of his former ferocity – that frightened me.

Pressing on, I said, 'There is Madam Florio. She is unleashed. She has no fear. She will have her say.'

'Then we are not alone.'

In answer, I merely returned his stare, allowing him to reach his own conclusion. After a brief interval, he shook his head at life's complexity, then continued pacing. After another pause he said, 'Now that we have put this matter aside, I consider also my Lord Burghley.'

'You have received word from him?' I asked.

'No, but I believe he stirs.'

'You have heard a report, perhaps?'

'The Privy Council extends the closure of London theatres for another year.'

'Even though the plague decreases?'

'I sense his cold hand in the decision. He would happily starve them unto death; or, failing that, drive them to destitution.'

'But if he is as cold, as calculating as you say, why would he act so passionately against so small and distant a threat?'

At this, my lord turned away. 'Oh, he is mortally insulted. He will consider where to strike. Perhaps he believes he has found my weakness.'

Turning his own attention once more to the flames, he continued to strike at the logs with the iron.

Chapter 23

I WALKED DOWN THE PASSAGEWAYS OF THE HOUSE, nodding to passers-by, as if in a dream, when Lucia turned a corner. She walked towards me, tall, slender, graceful, her demeanour open. Drawing broadside, she gave me a searching, powerful glance. I continued walking, not looking back, not daring to invoke that haughty strength. I heard nothing but my own deep breathing, rocked by the naked power of that look, like a small boat in another's wash. That night at my board I wrote:

O! call not me to justify the wrong
That thy unkindness lays upon my heart;
Wound me not with thine eye, but with thy tongue:
Use power with power, and slay me not by art.
Tell me thou lovest elsewhere; but in my sight,
Dear heart, forebear to glance thine eye aside:
What need'st thou wound with cunning, when thy might
Is more than my o'erpress'd defence can bide?
Let me excuse thee: ah! my love well knows
Her pretty looks have been mine enemies;
And therefore from my face she turns my foes,
That they elsewhere may dart their injuries:
   Yet do not so, but since I am near slain,
   Kill me outright with looks, and rid my pain.

Eating a midday meal in the great hall, I gnawed my meat, distracted by half-considered thoughts, dipping my other hand into the great earthen pot. My fingers, industrious, located a large potato which, splitting in two halves with my knife, I ate both swiftly and greedily. So poets wolf their food, unconscious of their

168

feeding. Thus engaged, I glanced absently down the table, until I saw – my fuller sight returning – something that struck me dumb.

My mind, as though distant, observed, ensconced at the other end of the table, the image of beauty incarnate. Lucia herself was not eating, but instead observing her own children, her expression calm and direct. Her husband Florio, that high-minded scholar and hater of poets, was engaged in feeding an infant – seated on his knee, pretty face upraised amongst the brood of four lusty children – with tender ministration. Amongst this family scene she seemed pale, composed, yet not unhappy. She did not look my way.

I wiped my mouth with the back of my hand and rose from my bench. I walked down the length of the hall, acknowledged Florio (though he barely acknowledged me) and moved briskly by him. Nothing, not a glance, passed between Lucia and myself. Perhaps she knew I intended then to crush our affair before it started. She, no doubt sensing my hardened will, merely looked away. Outside the dining hall, I drew in deep breath, was about to step forth when I was hailed from behind.

'Master Shakespeare!'

My lord approached me with his hand on the shoulder of another man, whom I recognised immediately.

'Our friend Master Marlowe has deigned to visit us. He takes temporary refuge from London.'

Master Marlowe and I bowed to one another in mock courtly ritual. My patron asked, turning to address me, 'Have you eaten?'

'I have.'

To Marlowe, my lord said, 'He scribbles unceasingly. He bolts his food and retires to his room.'

Marlowe shrugged laconically.

'Come, Master Marlowe, you will sit in his place.'

Marlowe smiled. The two of them entered the dining hall like old friends. But I watched them depart in an agony of apprehension, for there is nothing, perhaps even love, that makes a poet so jealous as another who threatens to cut off the light of his praise and sustenance.

Yet in addressing my rival, it was also something of a relief not to write of my own love, of my fiercest and obsessive passion. Sometimes a simple change of tone breathes light into a writer's circumstances. I could at least approach the task of writing about my fellow poet with a measure of irony.

In my room that night, I worked at my board, addressing my lord once more, scratching busily with my pen, pausing occasionally to read what I had written, then bending to my work again.

O! how I faint when I of you do write,
Knowing a better spirit doth use your name,
And in the praise thereof spends all his might,
To make me tongue-tied, speaking of your fame!
But since your worth – wide as the ocean is, –
The humble as the proudest sail doth bear,
My saucy bark, inferior far to his,
On your broad main doth wilfully appear.
Your shallowest help will hold me up afloat,
Whilst he upon your soundless deep doth ride:
Or, being wrack'd, I am a worthless boat,
He of tall building and of goodly pride.
Then if I thrive and I be cast away,
The worst was this; – my love was my decay.

Several days later, lost in thought, I walked through the garden in the main courtyard and saw my lord emerge from a doorway. He called out, 'My dear William, you have hidden yourself away.'

'You had a famous guest.'

'Master Marlowe? He is long departed. He visited but for a day. Now I wish to speak with you. There is something I should prefer to tell you in confidence. Perhaps you will be kind enough to pay a visit to my rooms this evening.'

I nodded, bowed, and we continued on our ways.

That evening, I did as he commanded, making my way along the paving stones of a passage on which a single rushlight burned. Its guttering light washed the walls. At the prospect of seeing him, I was perhaps a little lighter of heart than had been my usual diet over the last few days. As I approached the door to my lord's chambers, I heard sounds coming from within his room – the most common and yet the most unmistakable sounds. There was a high-pitched call, that might have been a woman's voice, and then the deeper groan of a man. Reaching the outside of that familiar door, I was like some vessel that passes along a river bank, about to touch the shore, but not yet touching. I slowed my walk, but did not halt as I passed the door. I even smiled to myself, for it seemed my young master had a female companion.

I am after all a man of the theatre, a somewhat raffish world. And since I am of a liberal disposition, why should I not be broad-minded about mistresses? I continued to walk, to float by on my current, though my ears listened. My momentum took me past the door. By now the sounds had ceased, as if the last seconds had been spent.

Amused at my lord's proclivities, and musing to myself, I was about to turn the corner, and return to my room, when I heard behind me the sound of a door being opened. I ducked into another passage. It was a good hiding place, well away from the flame that supplied the only illumination to that corridor. After a few moments, I put my head around the corner, then pulled back again, as someone from my lord's rooms emerged into the passageway. I heard, from the rising sound of footsteps, that the figure was walking towards me, so I withdrew further into darkness. The footsteps came closer. Like some night-creature, I pulled back yet further into the black.

A feminine shape with a strangely familiar profile passed. At its recognition I felt a terrible sickness come over me. Of those brief moments I remember nothing, except my pain, as I tried to swallow. The jaw hardens, and the mouth dries, though the mind seems oppressed. It was my own Lucia, Madam Florio, who walked past my hiding place – returning, no doubt, to her family. There was something precise and composed about her footsteps, something direct and almost wilful, and a strange intuition struck me then that perhaps it was not she who had been an entirely unwitting victim.

I felt crushed, as though a stone had been placed on my lungs. Like the animal I had become, I retreated to my room. I opened the door of my own small cell, leaned on the foot of my bed, fumbled with my hand along the shelf on which sat a few implements for eating. In my internal darkness I remember only knocking over several things which clattered to the floor. My searching, insensible fingers found a large wooden eating bowl, whose rim I gripped. I sat on the end of the bed, and was heartily sick into it.

When I finished retching, I put the bowl back on the stand, felt for my candleholder, raised myself, stepped outside the door, advanced to a nearby rushlight, lit my candle, returned to my room. The air inside seemed fetid. Ill with jealousy, I stood and opened a window, gazing out into empty darkness.

Setting the candle down so I could write on the board, I took up the quill, dipped it in ink, and for a while stared at the sheet of paper. I coughed once or twice, considered for a few moments, then began to write, hesitatingly at first:

Be wise as thou art cruel; do not press
My tongue-tied patience with too much disdain;

Lest sorrow lend me words, and words express
The manner of my pity-wanting pain.
If I might teach thee wit, better it were,
Though not to love, yet, love, to tell me so; —
As testy sick men when their deaths be near,
No news but health from their physicians know; —
For, if I should despair, I should grow mad,
And in my madness might speak ill of thee:
Now this ill-wresting world is grown so bad,
Mad slanderers by mad ears believed be.
  That I may be not so, nor thou belied,
  Bear thine eyes straight, though thy proud heart go
    wide.

Chapter 24

IN THE DINING HALL, seated at the great wooden table, I ate slowly and thoughtfully. Sometimes I glanced towards the end of the table. Lucia sat there with her young family, her husband Florio opposite her. She was helping her youngest child with food. Her other children played about her.

I turned back to my eating, staring ahead, then glanced back down the table again. Florio, no doubt wishing to return to his studies, was rising from the bench, leaning over to kiss his wife, patting one of the children on the head.

I returned to my eating. After a little while, I looked down the table once more. Florio had gone. Lucia was seated amongst her children. Now she answered my look with a direct stare. Deliberately, after holding my eyes, she moved her gaze towards a window that overlooked the garden outside. Even though I did not understand her full meaning, I gave a single nod, took in a deep breath, returned to my eating.

Outside, in the open air, I looked round at the empty gardens, glancing down one bare wall, then another. My attention halted and fixed on a point some fifty paces away where I could see the opening of an alcove, whose interior could not be seen from where I stood. I made my way towards it, glancing about me at the vacant spaces, before turning into the arbour.

Lucia rose from her seat. Before I could speak, she said, 'I know that it was you who saw me departing from my Lord Southampton's rooms.'

I felt an urge to draw back my hand to strike her, or perhaps to strike at my own fierce jealousy. But she pre-empted me, saying, 'Is that what I must do, sir, to gain your attention?'

Her expression was unflinching and defiant. I felt

the agony return. 'What would you have me do?' I asked.

Fiercely she answered, 'Meet me.'

'Where?'

She swept her arm around, towards the surrounding country. 'Spring has come. The trees are full of leaves.'

'Nature will hide our shame?'

'I have no shame,' she replied.

'And what of my Lord Southampton?'

'That is my own affair.'

I might have remonstrated with her, but she was implacable. Instead I indicated with a gesture the shallow hillside. 'Behind that hill is a woodland, and in that wood is a glade surrounded by several dense thickets. I sometimes walk there in the afternoon. It helps my composition.'

She looked up towards the hill. 'I will find an excuse to leave my duties. And I will find you, if you are to be found.'

I turned back to her. 'Now we must go. This place is more dangerous for you even than for me.'

But she seemed unafraid. 'Go first,' she said calmly, 'and I will follow when you are gone.'

That night I lay on my bed, the flame of the candle beside me. My mind was filled with the images of my love, and the peculiar circumstances by which, having attempted to prevent her husband from being dismissed, I was now the victim of my own charity. Meanwhile, I had struggled to express my own feelings through the only means that seemed open to the expression of my thoughts. I had begun the poem in fierce anger and exasperation at my plight, but what emerged in the course of a night of labour was more like pleading. Beside me, on the board, another page had been filled with verse.

> *Lo, as a careful housewife runs to catch*
> *One of her feather'd creatures broke away,*
> *Sets down her babe, and makes all swift dispatch*
> *In pursuit of the thing she would have stay;*
> *While her neglected child holds her in chase,*
> *Cries to catch her whose busy care is bent*
> *To follow that which flies before her face,*

Nor prizing her poor infant's discontent:
So runn'st thou after that which flies from thee,
Whilst I thy babe chase thee afar behind;
But if thou catch thy hope, turn back to me,
And play the mother's part, kiss me, be kind.
  So will I pray that thou mayst have thy Will,
  If thou turn back and my loud crying still.

I turned on my side and blew out the candle. In the dark I heard, as though beside me, the sounds of a woman crying out in pleasure. In my mind's eye, in that shadowy limit between sleeping and waking, Lucia and I rolled in the undergrowth, turning over and over languorously. It seemed to me that much of that spring and early summer passed like that dream, half way between darkness and light, one foot in heaven and another in hell. And so for several months I cuckolded Florio while my lord, in a manner of speaking, cuckolded me.

Chapter 25

I NOW HAD TWO RIVALS FOR MY MISTRESS – her own husband and my lord. Yet I continued to visit Master Florio's rooms in pursuit of his stored volumes on Italy, whose city states seemed increasingly appropriate as settings for my plays – despite his jibes about my ignorance. His own work, in the form of manuscripts, lay about the place, and since he gave me access to his scholarship – if only on the grounds that when I was in his rooms I would not be diverting my lord with my wasteful sonnets – I also perused his finished manuscripts for scholarship or learning of which I could make use. I noticed that in one of his own works John Florio had written that his ideal of feminine beauty was dark: dark hair, dark eyebrows, dark eyes. His own wife epitomised those views. Lucia was dark in those ways that he described, and since I felt a touch of spite or irony towards one who was so dismissive of poets, I used the theme as a constant to describe my beloved in the sonnets I was writing so fervently in the quiet secrecy of my room:

> In the old age black was not counted fair,
> Or if it were, it bore not beauty's name;
> But now is black beauty's successive heir,
> And beauty slander'd with a bastard shame:
> For since each hand hath put on Nature's power,
> Fairing the foul with Art's false borrow'd face,
> Sweet beauty hath no name, no holy bower,
> But is profan'd, if not lives in disgrace.
> Therefore my mistress' brows are raven black,
> Her eyes so suited, and they mourners seem
> At such who, not born fair, no beauty lack,

Sland'ring creation with a false esteem:
  Yet so they mourn, becoming of their woe,
  That every tongue says beauty should look so.

The tensions of living in that house, and pursuing my dark love, released a flood of composition and work in me. Writing about my beloved seemed to me a counterpoint to writing of my patron. In my lord's case, the agreement between us was that I would create a set of flowering praises based upon chaste love, according to the traditions of the sonnet. But this convention of continuous praise also acted as a kind of constraint on my writing. In composing upon my mistress I could do almost the opposite. I could list her attributes – even those which were not beautiful – with a realistic, fervent relish. The elegant inversion was that however beautiful my lord might be, I had no physical passion for him. However unremarkable my dark lady might be, my feelings towards her were suffused with fiercest and most holy desire. And what was stranger, perhaps, was that I could be certain that that most high and intelligent being, my patron, would approve of my disquisitions upon her charms.

My mistress' eyes are nothing like the sun;
Coral is far more red than her lips' red:
If snow be white, why then her breasts are dun;
If hairs be wires, black wires grow on her head.
I have seen roses damask'd, red and white,
But no such roses see I in her cheeks;
And in some perfumes is there more delight
Than in the breath that from my mistress reeks.
I love to hear her speak, yet well I know
That music hath a far more pleasing sound:
I grant I never saw a goddess go; –
My mistress, when she walks, treads on the ground:
  And yet, by heaven, I think my love as rare
  As any she belied with false compare.

However much I might attempt to separate my patron and my beloved in my mind, I could not help myself complaining of the affair between them. So my verse continued to pour out from me, taking this or that attitude, exploring this or that conceit. Beneath all my imagery lay a continuous excitation and pain. We each of us lived under the same roof, after all, and whereas both her husband and my lord could consort with my love in that household – the first by right as a husband and the second as *seigneur* in the privacy of his own apartments – I myself was forced to live on the periphery, like a scavenger or crow, pleading for assignations in the furthest gardens or nearest woodlands, which were difficult to achieve. For though my mistress could be seen openly carrying messages or documents between Master Florio and his young charge, she could not be seen to visit my own rooms. Addressing my lord, and the circumstances of our mutual love, at certain times I gritted my teeth and tried to make the best of it, attempting to place his own coupling with my beloved in a more detached frame.

Take all my loves, my love, yea, take them all;
What has thou then more than thou hadst before?

187

No love, my love, that thou mayst true love call;
All mine, was thine before thou hadst this more.
Then, if for my love thou my love receivest,
I cannot blame thee for my love thou usest;
But yet be blam'd, if thou thyself deceivest
By wilful taste of what thyself refusest.
I do forgive thy robbery, gentle thief,
Although thou steal thee all my poverty;
And yet, love knows it is a greater grief
To bear love's wrong than hate's known injury.
    Lascivious grace, in whom all ill well shows,
    Kill me with spites; yet we must not be foes.

Every hour of every day I struggled to keep a sense of perspective, and tried not to hate my patron. For even while he extended like an angel the hand of protection over me, gave me food and warmth and enough payment for my efforts to at least send to my own family in Stratford, yet the fact of his commingling with my beloved burned into my soul. I could not prevent my own bitterness from entering my verse, and addressing my mistress in wounded terms:

> *So, now I have confess'd that he is thine,*
> *And I myself am mortgag'd to thy will,*
> *Myself I'll forfeit, so that other mine*
> *Thou wilt restore, to be my comfort still:*
> *But thou wilt not, nor he will not be free,*
> *For thou art covetous, and he is kind;*
> *He learn'd but surety-like to write for me,*
> *Under that bond that him as fast does bind.*
> *The statue of thy beauty thou wilt take,*
> *Thou usurer, that putt'st forth all to use,*
> *And sue a friend came debtor for thy sake;*
> *So him I lose through my unkind abuse.*
> > *Him have I lost; thou has both him and me:*
> > *He pays the whole, and yet I am not free.*

And so the dance proceeded. Despite the double pain of knowledge and acquiescence, my mind continued obsessively to churn the theme, searching for different perspectives. Because my love for her was fierce and overwhelming, she was the one I could not forgive, and the one about whom my writing was harshest and most brutal. In my lord's case, it seemed to me that when one as fair and attractive as he was wooed or pursued by one as formidably alluring as my mistress, he was bound to succumb. So, while my hurting heart turned like an animal in its cage, my mind constructed further sonnets of praise to my patron:

> Those petty wrongs that liberty commits,
> When I am sometimes absent from thy heart,
> Thy beauty and thy years full well befits,
> For still temptation follows where thou art.
> Gentle thou art, and therefore to be won,
> Beauteous thou art, therefore to be assail'd;
> And when a woman woos, what woman's son
> Will sourly leave her till she have prevail'd?
> Ay me! but yet thou mightst my seat forbear,
> And chide thy beauty and thy straying youth,
> Who lead thee in their riot even there
> Where thou art forc'd to break a twofold truth,—

Hers, by thy beauty tempting her to thee,
Thine, by thy beauty being false to me.

Chapter 26

THROUGH THAT YEAR and into the winter, my mind continued to turn in its agony, even searching for hidden compensations in my circumstances:

> That thou hast her, it is not all my grief,
> And yet it may be said I lov'd her dearly;
> That she hath thee, is of my wailing chief,
> A loss in love that touches me more nearly.
> Loving offenders, thus I will excuse ye:
> Thou dost love her, because thou know'st I love her;
> And for my sake even so doth she abuse me,

Suffering my friend for my sake to approve her.
If I lose thee, my loss is my love's gain,
And losing her, my friend has found that loss;
Both find each other, and I lose both twain,
And both for my sake lay on me this cross:
 But here's the joy; my friend and I are one;
 Sweet flattery! then she loves but me alone.

There were other aspects of my circumstances that fretted at me, and to which I gave certain licence. I was entering my thirtieth year, and my patron and rival in love was not yet twenty. I could not help but compare our respective ages.

When my love swears that she is made of truth,
I do believe her, though I know she lies,
That she might think me some untutor'd youth,
Unlearned in the world's false subtleties.
Thus vainly thinking that she thinks me young,
Although she knows my days are past the best,
Simply I credit her false-speaking tongue:
On both sides thus is simple truth supprest.

But wherefore says she not she is unjust?
And wherefore say not I that I am old?
O! love's best habit is in seeming trust,
And age in love loves not to have years told:
  Therefore I lie with her and she with me,
  And in our faults by lies we flatter'd be.

However much I tried to balance the competing claims of the players in our drama, sometimes the strains were too much to bear, and I released my emotions in a stream of vitriol. In our common slang 'hell' was a synonym for the female sexual parts. In that respect I visited my own favourite hell as much as I could, and with an enthusiasm that over-rode all other considerations.

Two loves I have of comfort and despair,
Which like two spirits do suggest me still:
The better angel is a man right fair,
The worser spirit a woman, colour'd ill.

To win me soon to hell, my female evil
Tempteth my better angel from my side,
And would corrupt my saint to be a devil,
Wooing his purity with her foul pride.
And whether that my angel be turn'd fiend
Suspect I may, but not directly tell;
But being both from me, both to each friend,
I guess one angel in another's hell:
  Yet this shall I ne'er know, but live in doubt,
  Till my bad angel fire my good one out.

My lord had once said of me that I see clear and burn hot. Yet my mistress had dragged me out of my vaunted detachment, hauled me to my own hell. Sometimes, in moments of repose, my equilibrium would return. In order to assuage some sense of spirit, during her absence I began yet another sonnet.

For several days I had been tempted to write about the cost to the spirit of living so recklessly in the physical world, arguing that the very act of love and courtship was a poor return for the soul's investment.

The body itself would soon grow old and be eaten by worms. By turning away from that vain world, could not one buy better terms than to lose oneself entirely in the infernal delights of passion? Could not one feed oneself internally by contemplation, study, writing – perhaps by constructing some immemorial lines on the fallibility of all things physical?

Poor soul, the centre of my sinful earth,
Fool'd by these rebel powers that thee array,
Why dost thou pine within and suffer dearth,
Painting thy outward walls so costly gay?
Why so large cost, having so short a lease,
Dost thou upon thy fading mansion spend?
Shall worms, inheritors of this excess,
Eat up thy charge? Is this thy body's end?
Then, soul, live thou upon thy servant's loss,
And let that pine to aggravate thy store;
Buy terms divine in selling hours of dross;
Within be fed, without be rich no more:
    So shalt thou feed on Death, that feeds on men,
    And Death once dead, there's no more dying then.

It is one thing to write sonnets advocating ascetism and the inner life, another to live out that life with dedication. Soon I was drawn once more into that self-absorbed cycle of passion and repletion. Every thought has its counter-thought, and the vehemence of my mind was such that every counter-thought could be explored with equal ferocity and rigour. My prick, that dumb lover, too often led my spirit:

> Love is too young to know what conscience is;
> Yet who knows not conscience is born of love?
> Then, gentle cheater, urge not my amiss,
> Lest guilty of my faults thy sweet self prove:
> For, thou betraying me, I do betray
> My nobler part to my gross body's treason;
> My soul doth tell my body that he may
> Triumph in love; flesh stays no further reason;
> But, rising at thy name, doth point out thee
> As his triumphant prize. Proud of this pride,
> He is contented thy poor drudge to be,
> To stand in thy affairs, fall by thy side.
>   No want of conscience hold it that I call
>   Her 'love' for whose dear love I rise and fall.

It did not matter to me that we were both married, had good and faithful spouses, that I had three children by mine and she four by hers, the fact was that we broke our bed-vows constantly.

In loving thee thou know'st I am forsworn,
But thou art twice forsworn, to me love swearing;
In act thy bed-vow broke, and new faith torn
In vowing new hate after new love bearing.
But why of two oaths' breach do I accuse thee,
When I break twenty? I am perjur'd most;
For all my vows are oaths but to misuse thee,
All my honest faith in thee is lost:
For I have sworn deep oaths of thy deep kindness,
Oaths of thy love, thy truth, thy constancy;
And, to enlighten thee, gave eyes to blindness,
Or made them swear against the thing they see;
  For I have sworn thee fair; more perjur'd I,
  To swear against the truth so foul a lie!

Chapter 27

*I*T HAPPENED THAT MY LORD and I would ride out for exercise on most days, especially if a winter sun showed through. If I feared for his safety against the greater forces in the land, it also sometimes seemed to me that his precocious and scholarly mind moved ahead of my own. One day, while we rode together, he said, 'I sometimes am tempted to believe that life is nothing more than a comedy, a comedy of errors.'

'In what manner?' I asked.

'I think of my Lord Burghley, of his effect upon me. What if another guardian had been appointed after my father's death? I would not have been engaged by arrangement to Elizabeth de Vere, and the great fine that threatens me would now not overhang me. I would not have a tutor by the name of John Florio, or his wife living within my house. And I would not be engaged with his wife upon matters which set me at odds with a certain suitor of hers called Master Shakespeare, for whom I am happy to act as patron.'

We now seldom mentioned directly the subject of our mutual mistress. In truth I did not mind this much. In our silence was complicity, and perhaps a certain respect for the rights of the other. Besides which, he read my sonnets, continued to praise them avidly for their force and cogency, and through them at least knew enough of the turmoil of my mind.

Tentatively I asked, 'Of what aspect in particular do you think?'

I expected him to raise the matter of Florio, and perhaps of Florio's wife, but instead he answered, 'I think of the manner in which my Lord Burghley, having received my insult to his supervision of me, has not yet seen fit to respond. I think of his patience, while he waits his opportunity, and how each day he increases his threat by the act of withholding.'

'You do not think perhaps that we are subject to a false alarm?' I asked.

He smiled on me, kindly, but a little pityingly, as though perhaps I did not understand matters of honour between noblemen. 'You think that this is much ado about nothing, do you, Master Shakespeare?'

'You know the mind of my Lord Burghley better than I,' I conceded.

He smiled again, but said nothing, and so we continued on our journey in silence.

In winter the fires warmed the halls of that former monastery. We, its denizens, were often out upon our errands and obligations. Sometimes the freezing sea winds would cross the lea, cutting through clothes, touching the bone, chilling the fastnesses of garden. There we reclined, in fitful sunshine. So, exposed to fate, we found ourselves arrested in false calm, throwing no shadows, but filling the shallow industry of days. I myself, no less active by night than day, limned my private hours with furtive labour. So time passed, ending in exhausted sleep.

But just as storm clouds rising in the west appeared from nothing, a single speck or spark in the horizon's blue, so Lord Burghley's threat and presence lay across that house, bringing winter's cold to winter's fitful sunlight. The seasons changed in slow course. In spring, the white flowers we called snowdrops rose from the fields as pale as ghosts. We lived in a dilapidated sun, which brought us light, but kept us from the warmth.

I continued to work upon my plays, hoping for that time when the threat of plague would be lifted from the theatres, and I could earn my living once more from entertaining the restless London crowds. If nothing else, the forced interval allowed me to review my own past work, to consider my own salient weaknesses and occasional strengths.

As I laboured on new schemes and plays, it seemed to me that if there was an emptiness in my own drama, it lay with schemers, machiavels, and birds of ill passage. Their drive towards evil I failed to understand.

My answer was to clothe them in darkness, in grand mystery, removing their motive, and by so doing magnify their intent. By dissolving their motive, I both solved and resolved their ambition.

If I am a countryman, lover of earth and women, respecter of the seasons, sceptical of religion and all abstractions, my lack of a grand design means that I cannot help but offer sympathy to every character. In my own mind each living thing that moves upon the world strives to perfect itself. If I make a common thief he shall be the finest thief that I can imagine – the most wicked and full of pathos. Thus my emerging characters, conforming to no special design, and almost by the accident of my own lack of a philosophy, seem to stand out from their surrounds, becoming the agents of nothing but themselves.

My great peer and rival, Marlowe, by contrast, gave his darkness motive. Faustus sold his soul for worldly goods, Tamburlaine for an earthly crown. Darkness was a poetic sublime, always present; darkness as deft line on hourglass day, darkness as faint image in stained glass, darkness as incarmined rose. Darkness was close with him, was in certain respects his familiar. In other aspects I could match him, perhaps even overcome him – in subtlety rather than strength, in the complexity of an individual's inner life, in the myriad motives within that individual's deepest self. But I would never match the almost voluptuous movement of his soul towards ultimate perdition. And perhaps that was why I would never write a play to match the hell-conjuring *Faustus*, that great and wilful supplicant of eternal damnation.

It seemed to me – who did not know Marlowe well – that he was drawn towards darkness as others were drawn towards light. He was the great Lucifer of our drama – atheist, philosopher, diplomat, spy, lover of men, goad of authority, implacable in his confidence and arrogance. Beneath my own amiable rivalry and admiration was a deeper fear: that he could entrance the mind of my patron, encourage him to stare over the precipice, entice him not so much to hell as to a romantic self-destruction. So I watched nervously as the great poet visited my lord's house occasionally through the seasons, conferred at length with my patron, and mysteriously came and went.

Winter mists moved across the land and, pale as ghosts, were blown across winter fields. By simple fervour of mind, it sometimes seemed to me, I held the world at bay. My own thoughts were delicate deer on mind's horizon. I used to live with an ear to the line of communal earth, surviving like a ghost myself, outside London, writing my work in the recesses of a great house, absorbing information where I could about the political movements of the day, hoping one day to return to the stage.

Chapter 28

WHILE WINTER HAD LASTED, it at least had held one advantage. The removal of foliage from the trees meant that one could survey the land more easily. It became correspondingly more difficult for horsemen or watchers to hide in our proximity. When I travelled with my lord to his early morning swims at the lake, I could look about the land, knowing that no horsemen were concealed in the neighbouring bare woods.

Yet when spring returned, and foliage appeared once more on the trees, I again became nervous. Even when golden sunshine dappled the earth, and the birds began to sing, I surveyed the surrounding country, the rolling hills, the verdant woods, searching for any sign of the horsemen who had haunted us the previous year. For the time being I could see nothing, only our companionable shadows. Our horses trotted, neighbourly and calm, side by side along the beaten track. Light fell in palpable, bright sentences through the early foliage of trees.

My apprehension remained with me. Yet it was only when I was riding on my own that I became most fully aware of the danger. On one occasion my lord was away for several days in London attending to his duties at court; and so, after a night of working at my board, followed by brief, fitful sleep, the following morning I saddled and rode out into the countryside alone.

Several furlongs from the house, I turned around a corner of hillside, and observed unexpectedly three bulking shadows beside a small stream, three horses drinking shadow. In that clearing the horsemen who sat on their animals' backs were armed as if for war, with chain mail and with long swords sheathed in scabbards. They were in restful state, turning to observe my approach while their horses drank and they talked casually amongst themselves. But unlike my Lord

Southampton, who might have challenged them, interrogating their presence in his woods, I shrank back from the sight of them, not wishing even to draw close. Instead I swung my horse as deftly as I could down another path, which, to my good fortune, led along a gully and so removed me from their immediate sight. Nervously, I strained to hear whether, curious at my sudden diversion, they would follow me. Perhaps they suspected I was the indigent poet and playwright who accompanied the young earl and who – according to Master Florio – led him astray. On my own, without my lord's protection, I was someone they could kill easily, as easily as snapping the spine of some small bird or animal. There would have been no evidence either, just a dead man lying in the forest leaf-litter and a nervous horse cropping the grass nearby. Perhaps my playwright's mind was too filled with the images of murder.

Carefully, while following the path along that gully, I swung my horse onto the mossy verge, where its hooves would make less sound than on the stony path. It seemed to my alarmed mind that those three horse-men were less likely to hear me break into a canter, then a gallop, as I rode fast through the woodland towards the protection of the great house. Only when I came within sight of its chimneys, and could be viewed from its windows, did I consider myself safe, at least on that day. A part of me was still fearful, was listening to the sound of hoofbeats behind me. But no sound came. I slowed my horse to a trot, and then to a walk, as my swiftly pounding heart subsided.

Chapter 29

DESPITE THE THREAT FROM HORSEMEN, it was still my custom, waiting for my love, to seat myself on a rudimentary bench in a certain clearing in the woods a mile or so distant from the house. One day, positioned there, I was lost in contemplation. A breeze moved the grass and the leaves on the trees. Glancing up, I caught sight of a figure approaching along the path, in a hood and dark cloak. When the figure drew closer I saw that it was Lucia, now standing tall and slender in front of me, the hood still covering most of her face.

I stood up and faced her. Tenderly I drew back the hood, drawing in my breath sharply. The side of her face was a dark, heavy bruise. I shuddered with horror, but Lucia looked with fierce calm into my eyes.

'It is my husband. He has found me out.'

'My sweet – ' I began, but she interceded.

'I need no sympathy. It is less than I expected. In his own country there is a law that a man may kill his wife out of passion if she is faithless.'

'He has spied on us?' I asked.

'No,' – still with that peculiar, settled calm, as though speaking of the weather – 'not on us. On my Lord Southampton.'

My turmoil took a different shape.

'You should beware,' I said. 'Your husband has the ferocity and discipline of a scholar.'

'Oh, he is rigorous,' she said. 'Yet he will not harm me any further in my lord's household. It would shame his master.'

But I persisted, 'What would happen if he should discover us?'

She replied, with apparent unconcern, 'He would have killed me for certain. Not only for my unfaithfulness, but because he despises poets above everything.'

Despite our circumstances, I could not help but smile. At the same I time felt obliged to mitigate my mirth. 'Forgive me, my sweet. This is no time for levity at our predicament.'

But she was smiling too, rare and beautiful. 'Oh, it is the very time for mirth. To him, the work of poets is nothing but a useless absurdity. He says of your poems that they are the "lost labours" of love. I believe he has used precisely this phrase to my Lord Southampton in admonishing him for wasting his time on such things.'

'The lost labours of love,' I repeated. 'He hath the tongue of a poet himself.' Some of my mirth left me. 'He is certain of matters ... between you and my lord?'

She swallowed and nodded.

I stroked her hair, and said tenderly, 'Then I can risk your life no longer.'

She stared back at me. 'I do not regret one moment, my one and only love.'

I returned her tender stare. 'And what of his lordship?'

'I will continue. It is now the only thing which keeps my husband in employment.'

215

I marvelled again at her perspicacity. 'If your husband were dismissed, my Lord Burghley would surely employ him.'

'No. His use to my Lord Burghley is as a spy. Without that he would lack all utility.'

'But his scholarship – '

'My Lord Burghley makes a distinction between a scholar and a poet, it is true. But he finds no other use for scholars than to pursue his ends.'

'Yet you protect your husband, even though – ' I could not help but look at the brutal bruises on her face.

'He is a good father. He needs me for the children.'

'That will be your life?'

'Now that our love is over, I will protect my family as I know best.'

Bereft of words, I put my arms around her, and held her close to me, crushed my face to her neck, felt the agony overcome me.

Chapter 30

 THE LIFE OF A POET IS STRANGE; haunted by fear, ransacked by loathing at the workings of this false world, yet also sometimes steeped in admiration for those who are able to walk its crooked paths without being corrupted. While I burned with jealousy at my love's continuation with my Lord Southampton, at the same time I perceived something admirable in her steadfastness to both him and me, which did not cause me to lose my desire, but if anything increased it. I worked at my table, writing a line of verse, pausing, writing another.

Thine eyes I love, and they, as pitying me,
Knowing thy heart torments me with disdain,
Have put on black and loving mourners be,
Looking with pretty ruth upon my pain.
And truly not the morning sun of heaven
Better becomes the grey cheeks of the east,
Nor that full star that ushers in the even,
Doth half that glory to the sober west,
As those two mourning eyes become thy face:
O! let it then as well beseem thy heart
To mourn for me, since mourning doth thee grace,
And suit thy pity like in every part.
  Then will I swear beauty herself is black,
  And all they foul that thy complexion lack.

Chapter 31

I CONTINUED TO FREQUENT THOSE WOODS and glades
where we had made love, haunted them like a spectre.
Above me the raucous crows cawed. One day, staring at
the ground in deepest thought, in the distance I heard
the faint neighing of a horse, the jingle of a bridle, then
sounds of footsteps, feet sloughing in leaf-litter. In my
reverie I heard, closer now, yet still as though in some
distant part of me, a hoof stamp as a waiting horse fed
on grass. I was too preoccupied to notice, until a gloved
rider's hand was laid firmly on my shoulder.

I looked up to face my lord, looking down on me.

'Master William,' he said. 'Thou should not be too
morbid.'

He looked around at the landscape, at the crows, maddened in the treetops. 'I have seen you sitting here on several occasions now. It suits your mood?'

I shrugged, but did not answer.

My lord pointed behind him to where two horses stood, patiently grazing. 'I thought perhaps I might find you here. I have brought a spare mount, so that I may invite you to ride with me.'

'Ride?'

'Let us go to the coast. It is only a mile or two, and we will be alone. I want to speak with you on an important matter, away from this place and its damned conspiracies.' He gestured with his arm to indicate the direction of the house and its grounds.

So it was that, despite my reluctance to leave my accustomed post, I agreed to accompany him. We both mounted our horses, turned away and rode, through wood and meadow, until we reached the coast of the Solent. There we paused, and looked out upon the green sea, towards the louring island, where the gulls spun in the sun and wind like flakes of gold.

My lord dismounted at a small wood on the edge of the water. I followed suit. We tethered our horses to the stunted oak trees along the edge of that wind-shriven shore, and together we walked towards the small beach where the breeze sang over the sand. There we stood looking out over the sea.

My lord said, 'I like to see the breeze upon the Solent, the boats moving under sail, and behind them the sun falling about the hills of the Isle of Wight. When I was a child, I would imagine the island was some foreign country.'

Several large stones or boulders stood nearby. My lord sat down on one of them. He seemed curiously weary at first, not inclined to speak. Then he said, 'As you know, I have been to London in the last few days, to attend to my duties as a peer. Our capital is aflame with reports and rumours. The Privy Council, under my Lord Burghley, has issued a warrant for the arrest of Christopher Marlowe and Thomas Kyd, on charges of atheism and heresy.'

At first I was struck silent by the news. These were my brothers in the scribbling arts, my most admired peers. I recall stammering, 'Why? Our two greatest dramatists – '

My lord interrupted me, speaking in cold, clipped

sentences which perhaps hid his own anguish. 'Marlowe has protectors and is on bail, but Kyd is arrested. They say that Kyd has already been racked, and that Marlowe will soon follow.'

Horror touched my insides. I said, 'Kyd is made of sweetness. He is called "sporting Kyd". He would not willingly offend against anyone.'

'Broken-backed, on his bed, crying his confession.'

I put my head in my hands. My lord said, 'Marlowe is made of harsher stuff. They say he defies the Privy Council to arrest him, that as a spy for the Walsinghams he yet knows about certain things which under torture he would reveal. There are matters which would perhaps bring down some of the great with him, including perhaps the younger Walsingham, who inherits the mantle of the old spymaster.'

A sudden anger gripped me. 'Who drives this?' I asked. 'Who is so motivated to destroy a few harmless songbirds – ?'

'My Lord Burghley,' he interrupted me. 'Our great, puritan Lord Burghley, chief minister in the Privy Council, who, if he could, would abolish all the arts, save the art of conspiracy. My Lord Burghley, to whom my tutor Master Florio is in thrall, sends out his cold message to me, his ward, to mend my ways and to desist from the company of poets.'

The pattern of it became clearer. In my confusion I enquired of my youthful master, as though he might hold the answer to these unfolding events, 'And what will you do now?'

To my surprise he smiled at me, a strange soft smile, as though he foresaw his own destiny.

'I am the third Earl of Southampton. My grandfather, the first Earl, was a greater statesman than Burghley. You think I shall be intimidated?'

'Even so, my Lord, would you not do well to proceed cautiously.'

'In what manner?' he asked.

'Perhaps,' I suggested tentatively, 'it would be better if I should leave your house.'

'Only the fearful proceed cautiously,' he replied. 'As for your proposal, sir, I have this to say: do what you do best, Master Shakespeare. Continue to sing like a bird. And allow me the task of responding to my Lord Burghley, one thing for another, measure for measure.'

What he said had been asserted with peculiar confidence. And not for the first time on that strange and melancholy day, I perceived perhaps that the youth was changing into the man.

I persisted as best I could in my concern. 'Is Marlowe entirely beyond our help? What I mean, my lord, is that I would leave your house if you felt you could offer him protection in my stead.'

He stood up and faced out to sea. But he seemed distracted. I said, 'Marlowe needs your protection more than I do.'

'You have spoken well,' he replied at last. 'But I doubt if he would accept my offer. Besides, now that Kyd and Marlowe are both disarmed, I believe I have a duty to protect you.'

Something in his answer caused me to pause. 'Marlowe is gone, too?'

'I believe it in my bones.' He still stared out to sea.

For myself I could not help a touch of irony at his certainty, 'You foresee the future, perhaps?'

If he noticed my sarcasm, he ignored it. Instead he said, 'It is dangerous, dangerous beyond the point of recklessness, for Master Marlowe to threaten to expose his master Walsingham if he himself should be tortured.'

'Why? What alternative has he?'

He shook his head at my naïveté. 'Cannot you see? My Lord Burghley has arranged circumstances so that either Walsingham or Marlowe will be revealed. Like a skilful hunter, he drives them both towards the same trap. The younger Walsingham will only survive if Marlowe dies.' He turned towards me. 'My Lord Burghley has set the pieces of his machinery in position. The engine of events will now take its course.'

I should have kept quiet, but his confident assertions seemed to goad me. I said, 'You know something more than you have said, perhaps?'

A sound like a sigh escaped him. 'There is a rumour now abroad that a certain great poet, while staying in a low tavern at Deptford, entered an argument with his companions over who would pay the bill of fare.'

He continued speaking in his low, calm voice, and while he talked the place that he described became vivid for me, and my mind constructed the scene.

Chapter 32

CHRISTOPHER MARLOWE SAT in a tavern with several companions. Even my lord's mention of their names caused a shudder to run through me – Ingram Frizer, Robert Poley and Nicholas Skeres – the very same stalwarts and torturers who accompanied the younger Walsingham when he accosted me in a passageway of my lord's house.

The four of them sat round a table, throwing dice, until the turn passed to Master Marlowe himself. He slipped the two cubes into a little cup, rattled them, and threw them on the table, saying, 'Fate obeys me tonight.'

The dice passed on to Poley, who shook them and threw casually. While the dice passed around the table, Frizer spoke in a soft, insinuating voice. 'It is said, Master Marlowe, that you threaten to expose our master Walsingham if the Privy Council have a mind to put you on the rack.'

'Indeed, Master Frizer,' Marlowe replied. 'Since torture searches one's innards, it would be difficult not to say what one knows, or not to intimate what one has seen.'

'And what has one seen?' Frizer asked.

'One has seen, for example, our master Walsingham's interest in certain young men, and one has witnessed his subsequent enjoyment of them.'

It was Frizer's turn to throw the dice. At the same time he said calmly, 'One should not throw stones in a glass house, so it is said.'

'You misunderstand me,' Marlowe replied. 'I do not criticise our master. On the contrary, I praise him. I merely state what I have seen.'

'Even so,' Frizer persisted, 'it is said that, since you have the same tastes, the pot should not call the kettle black.'

Marlowe observed the dice, smiling ironically, replying, 'They that like not tobacco and boys are fools.'

Around the table the other men smiled to themselves. At the same Frizer, softly insistent, said, 'You have not answered my question.'

'What question is that?' asked Marlowe.

'You intend to speak of what you have seen?'

'That is precisely the point, Master Frizer. Under torture these fine distinctions will cease to matter. All will be revealed. That is the thought which properly exercises our master Walsingham.'

'And you think this will save you?' Frizer asked.

Marlowe appeared outwardly calm while he threw the dice again. 'Our master will strive to save himself, and therefore he will strive his utmost to save me.'

The others continued to pass around the dice. At that stage, perhaps, Frizer glanced over at the somewhat burly landlord, who was dipping tankards in a bowl of water, wiping them with a rag, and setting them up on a shelf. The landlord nodded and, taking his time – as though in answer to Frizer's look – walked over to the doorway. He closed the wooden door and set the heavy crossbar down firmly across it.

Perhaps Marlowe noticed the arcane communication between Frizer and the landlord, for he commented, 'I have a sense, Master Frizer, that you are a denizen of this locality.'

'I am a citizen of Deptford, it is true.'

'Our master Walsingham prizes the citizens of Deptford,' Marlowe said. 'He informed me of it personally.'

'How did he express himself?'

'He told me,' Marlowe added, throwing the dice again, 'that they were the scurviest knaves in the kingdom, and if he ever wanted as mean and low a torturer's assistant as he could find, why, Deptford was the place to find him.'

Having secured the door, the landlord approached the table casually behind the speaker, standing silent, as though witnessing the throw of dice. Suddenly, without warning, he seized Marlowe from behind and pulled him backwards. At the same time, as though animated by the same impulse, Poley and Skeres leapt up from their seats and seized the poet by each of his arms.

Marlowe struggled, kicked and twisted, but he

could not break their grip. The fiercely struggling group moved back until they struck one of the walls. Frizer followed them, carrying one of the chairs. There they forced their victim into a seated position.

Frizer reached into his pocket and pulled out a dirty leather bundle. From it he unsheathed a knife with a long blade.

He advanced on Marlowe, saying, 'Our master Walsingham asked me to say one thing to you – that the eye is what it sees.'

With this, he plunged the knife into Marlowe's right eye, into the brain. The dying man gave a terrible scream, his body shuddered, his feet kicked spasmodically. The others held him until his struggles had ceased, and he was finally still.

Together they laid the body out on one of the long stout tables, even though Marlowe's legs still twitched.

Now Frizer rose – smooth, insinuating Frizer – addressing the landlord, enquiring, 'Tell me what you saw.'

The landlord said, 'I gave a reckoning of what was owed, but this gentleman lying here saw fit to debate the bill. And I said, who should settle it but him? And when it was pointed out what was owing, and that he should pay it, he pulled out a knife, so that what happened, happened.'

'And what might that be?'

'In the struggle which followed, that same knife entered his eye by accident.'

'You swear by this?' Frizer asked.

'On my life,' the landlord said.

Frizer withdrew a bag full of coins. 'And these pieces of silver?'

'I never saw them in my life.'

Frizer placed the money in the landlord's palm. The landlord's heavy fist closed over them.

'You see them now?' Frizer asked.

'To my eye, they are invisible.'

'Remember, if a word of this passes out, we will all swing together.'

'Of that I have no doubt,' the landlord said.

Chapter 33

*W*HEN THE DETAILS OF HIS STORY had been recounted, my Lord Southampton placed his hand on my shoulder. I shuddered, since I was still in the tavern of my own imagination.

For long afterwards, I would hear different accounts of the same event, all conflicting, all agreeing on only one thing – that Marlowe had been killed in a brawl in Deptford. A certain darkness, it seemed to me, lay over that part of London.

My lord said quietly, 'It is time we returned.'

That night I wrote at my board by the light of a single candle:

Was it the proud full sail of his great verse,
Bound for the prize of all too precious you,
That did my ripe thoughts in my brain inhearse,
Making their tomb the womb wherein they grew?
Was it his spirit, by spirits taught to write
Above a mortal pitch, that struck me dead?
No, neither he, nor his compeers by night
Giving him aid, my verse astonished.
He, nor that affable familiar ghost
Which nightly gulls him with intelligence,
As victors, of my silence cannot boast;
I was not sick of any fear from thence:
But when your countenance fill'd up his line,
Then lack'd I matter; that enfeebled mine.

When I had finished, I leaned back and stared past the candle into the blackness. At the same time, I could not help but whisper softly to myself, 'The better poet died. The lesser poet survived.'

Chapter 34

ALMOST ANOTHER YEAR PASSED, and during that time I remained like a nervous creature in my patron's household, hoping that my Lord Burghley's cold hand would not reach towards me too, and pluck me out. I continued to work in my cell through the autumn and the following frozen winter, writing and arranging my sonnets, attending to my plays, sometimes stepping out into thin spring sunshine for brief exercise.

I was fortunate to be absorbed by my labours. The acceptance that my love affair with my mistress was at an end was cruelly underlined by her continuation of relations with my patron. I could not blame her directly, for she herself had been entirely honest in the matter. She would persist with him, not least for the sake of her husband's position. Sometimes, though, my bitterness turned directly towards my lord, whose serene detachment over my predicament at times seemed to me like coldness, even heartlessness. It was only because I trusted him, and he trusted some sincerity in me, that I could write a poem which, though full of praises, yet had a vicious sting in its tail.

> They that have power to hurt and will do none,
> That do not do the thing they most do show,
> Who, moving others, are themselves as stone,
> Unmoved, cold, and to temptation slow;
> They rightly do inherit heaven's graces,
> And husband nature's riches from expense;
> They are the lords and masters of their faces,
> Others but stewards of their excellence.
> The summer's flower is to the summer sweet,
> Though to itself it only live and die;
> But if that flower with base infection meet,
> The basest weed outbraves his dignity:

For sweetest things turn sourest by their deeds;
Lilies that fester smell far worse than weeds.

A part of me desired to provoke him into some denial of heartlessness, or at least to account for his imperious detachment. Yet instead of reacting against my strictures on his coldness, he absorbed my criticism equally and without argument. So we continued in our own relations without further direct discussion of his perpetuation of relations with Madam Florio. It was as though he understood my tortured frustrations, but at the same time regarded them as peculiarly my own, and was unwilling to pander to them. I sensed too that he considered his greater responsibility lay in protecting me, and for that at least I continued to remain unfailingly grateful.

Perhaps I also misunderstood him, or at least the direction of his mind. For he was changing too, turning away from the more obvious pleasures of the world. It appeared to me that he was sinking deeper into his own thoughts and preoccupations. It was not so much that he had tired of constantly acting a single role – that of a glowing and gilded youth – but rather that he was in the process of growing into something else. By various means the heavy fine which hung over him now began to exert its effect. Perhaps he perceived that as the time of his payment approached, he would be forced by circumstances to live less magnificently.

I gained the impression that he calculated that he would be able to pay his fine in full, while at the same time keeping the main body of his lands and estate. The consequence was that on reaching his majority, he would be obliged to live more frugally. In anticipation of that fact, he had already begun to shed the trappings of earthly arrogance and power. The virtuous respond to their strictures by shriving their souls.

Perhaps he also perceived my perplexity at the changes in him. Our closer and more intimate discussions took place usually on horseback, when we were out of earshot of those in his house, such as John Florio, who might spy upon him. One day, as we rode through the country, he handed to me, without speaking, a parchment on which certain sentences had been scribbled in his hand. At the time we were on level terrain, and while my horse walked beside his, I was able to read the jottings. The first paragraph was set out in verse:

Rising each day, we think of the fallen.
Sleeping by night, we dream of the risen.
When the dawn is like a funeral pyre
I think of him in the time-honoured days –
Of one who was braver, more arrogant
Than ever hero lived, or wielded sword –
Fearless in confrontation, unflinching
In deed

The farewell he had begun seemed to end there. Another verse was begun below that, as though he were trying for a different metre and expression, following that of the person he mourned:

Brave, arrogant Marlowe, our much-lamented dead,
Had swept all before him, his over-reaching mind
Forming our new theatre, the tragic hero's tread
Stamping his impression on the public boards.

With something of a surprise, I saw my own name mentioned next, as though by contrast.

Calm, philosophic Shakespeare, far less bold
Moved beneath the surface, like some private spirit
Tightening his metre, rescinding rhetoric;
Though force might be lost, made up in subtle beauty.
To his task he brought an actor's precision,
Could turn and pivot with perfect timing,
Making rhythm dance, creating new forms
Of myriad diversity.

Beneath that was a final set of jottings, as though my patron were following his thoughts to some form of conclusion:

Though he may not possess Marlowe's thunder
Or his infernal sense of the sublime,
Yet by living within his creations
They emerge like true beings on the stage.

There the lines ended. They were not poems so much as private musings, thoughts caught on the wing.

Yet though they were somewhat rough, I could see in them the clear workings of my patron's mind. His consideration of the difference between the single beacon of Marlowe's genius and my own more pragmatic and varied talents seemed to me perceptive and not unfair.

At some level I believe Marlowe's death had affected my patron deeply, for the most profound changes occurred in him after the news of the great poet's decease. I did not know of the full nature of the companionship between them, and could not be certain if perhaps Marlowe had been his lover. If it were so, my patron had responded to his companion's death not by ostentatious lamentation, but with that cold and private solitude with which the strongest amongst us receive the worst news. My sense of intuition at the depth of his loss made my respect for him, if anything, the greater.

Chapter 35

My PATRON INSISTED that I stay under his protection for as long as I wished. But one day in late spring two horsemen rode up a shallow hillside overlooking the Earl of Southampton's great house.

Smoke poured from the chimneys. With the house behind us, we two riders approached the summit of that shallow hill – that hill which had become familiar to me in a previous summer, when leaves covered my assignations. Reaching the brow, my host turned his horse so that he faced me.

'Well, Master Shakespeare, I shall miss your company. But since the worst of the plague is over, and the theatres open again, it seems you are called once more to London.'

He was silent, patting his horse's mane.

I said, 'Lord Hunsdon has settled his theatre company for the new season. He calls it "The Lord Chamberlain's Men". I believe I will have employment there.'

'He charges you to write new plays?'

'I have several new plays for his eyes,' I replied, 'written during the plague years, while I enjoyed your patronage.'

'Remind me of them,' my lord requested.

'*The Taming of the Shrew, Richard III, Love's Labour's Lost.*'

He smiled at this, looking up at the sky as though in private enjoyment.

'So it is true,' he said finally aloud. 'You stole one of your titles from Master Florio, as he rightly maintains.'

'I am a magpie, my lord. Whatever shines, I will pilfer.'

He paused in amused contemplation. 'Your motto, then, is that the end justifies the means. All's well that ends well.'

'Precisely phrased,' I said.

Slowly, his expression became more serious. 'I have considered what best I might do to proceed against my Lord Burghley. For the time being, I will obey your advice, and keep Master Florio under my roof. Amongst other things, I owe it to his wife.'

I nodded my appreciation. He continued, 'But I have also considered, most calmly and carefully, how best I might strike back against my guardian. To that end, I have taken the trouble to purchase, for a round thousand pounds, a share in your name in Lord Hunsdon's company. I hope and believe that it will secure you against an uncertain future.'

My breath left me in contemplation of his act. It was an enormous sum. I said, mumbling incoherently, 'But you can ill afford – '

'I will survive,' he said, 'even after I have paid my great fine to my guardian. But afterwards, I will have the satisfaction of knowing that every success you make, every great and small entertainment, every poem or play that registers its force or felicity upon the mind of the public, will offend my Lord Burghley to his deepest soul.'

Tears started involuntarily in my eyes. I spoke, or stammered, 'A poet's life is no longer than a songbird's. If I could thank you for keeping me alive ... '

He seemed amused at this flood of emotion, and merely shrugged. Then he paused, and added, 'No gratitude is necessary, sir. Which of us truly knows his own future? Now, be gone with you. And do your work.'

I attempted to smile, but the tears were pouring uncontrollably down my cheeks. To hide my embarrassment, I started my horse. And so it was, approaching early summer, I rode away from my lord, blinded by both grief and gratitude.

When I turned to wave my final goodbye, he had already swung his horse and was riding back to his house, which for so long had been my home and refuge.

Chapter 36

I LOOK BACK NOW, at the end of my life, upon those times. During the plague years of 1592 to 1594, when the London theatres were closed, almost an entire generation of my fellow playwrights perished, amongst them Robert Greene, Thomas Kyd and Christopher Marlowe. Others, such as George Peele and Thomas Nashe, died not long afterwards of poverty.

On that late spring day, when my lord had announced the gift of an investment that would bolster me against the vicissitudes of my calling for the remainder of my life, I gave him in return a folded letter, which he acknowledged merely with a nod, and tucked into his clothes before he rode away.

In the course of my final message to him, I thanked him from my heart for his courtesy and generosity. At the end of that letter, like a *post scriptum*, I included one final poem. He had been utterly steadfast to me, through every adversity, through the attention of greater poets and the turmoil of our own passionate rivalry over a certain dark lady. And so it happened that the poem I passed to him on that day was my own paean to Platonic love.

Let me not to the marriage of true minds
Admit impediments. Love is not love
Which alters when it alteration finds,
Or bends with the remover to remove:
O, no! It is an ever-fixed mark,
That looks on tempests and is never shaken,
It is the star to every wandering bark,
Whose worth's unknown, although his height be taken.
Love's not Time's fool, though rosy lips and cheeks
Within his bending sickle's compass come;

Love alters not with his brief hours and weeks,
But bears it out even to the edge of doom.
If this be error, and upon me prov'd,
I never writ, nor no man ever lov'd.

In that final year I had not often seen my beloved, only in brief glimpses on her duties with her family, when she appeared both preoccupied and distracted. She seemed to have returned to her role as mother of her four children, a distant and remote figure inhabiting the same household. As my departure to London drew nearer, I did not attempt to write to her, since it would have risked her husband's wrath. But one day, as we passed one another in the rose garden, without speaking or embracing (for we might have been overlooked) I took the opportunity to hand to her a fair copy of a poem which I kept about my person. Hardly pausing, she slipped it carefully into her sleeve, though she smiled briefly at me – the first smile she had given me for many months – before walking on.

The poem would form the last of my sequence of a hundred and fifty-four sonnets. Its subject was desire itself. Despite every anguish and impediment, passion lived amongst us, not by sweetness and delight, but by the deepest and purest designs of our being. In one as sceptical as myself, I would choose to end my stream of sonnets on the subject of the perpetual fever of love, not as the harbinger of peace or wisdom, but expressed in the form of its own fire.

The little Love-god lying once asleep
Laid by his side his heart-inflaming brand,
Whilst many nymphs that vow'd chaste life to keep
Came tripping by; but in her maiden hand
The fairest votary took up that fire
Which many legions of true hearts had warm'd;
And so the general of hot desire
Was, sleeping, by a virgin hand disarm'd.
This brand she quenched in a cool well by,
Which from Love's fire took heat perpetual,
Growing a bath and healthful remedy

For men diseas'd; but I, my mistress' thrall,
　Came here for cure, and this by that I prove,
　Love's fire heats water, water cools not love.

Biographical Note

HENRY WRIOTHESLEY, the third Earl of Southampton, became a leading soldier and military commander who participated in numerous campaigns. He was a close ally of Queen Elizabeth's favourite, Robert Devereux, Earl of Essex. In 1598 Southampton, shortly before his twenty-fifth birthday, secretly married one of the Queen's maids of honour, Elizabeth Vernon, who was pregnant with his child. The marriage, which enraged the Queen (her maids of honour were meant to be maids) was considered a happy one, and produced several children. In 1601 Southampton was imprisoned in the Tower for his role in Essex's unsuccessful *coup d'état* against Elizabeth. Essex was executed. Southampton was eventually released from imprisonment on the accession of James I and restored to court. In 1624 Southampton died of fever while on military expedition in the Low Countries; his eldest son died with him, also of fever, in the same campaign.

William Shakespeare died peacefully in 1616, in Stratford-upon-Avon.

Afterword

ANYONE WHO ATTEMPTS TO WRITE on the subject of Shakespeare's sonnets approaches these great and mysterious works with considerable trepidation.

My own chief interest in writing *The Sonnets* was not so much to attempt to explore the social or physical world in which Shakespeare lived, as the landscape of his mind – the mind that produced his unprecedented body of work and which is, to some extent, revealed to us most directly in the poems themselves.

Given this background, it seemed to me that my approach should be to attempt to create a narrative frame for as many of Shakespeare's sonnets as could reasonably be incorporated (eventually some thirty-two of the poems were used) and to allow those sonnets – each reproduced in full – a leading role in creating that 'colour'.

In the course of working on the narrative of *The Sonnets* there were, however, two clear exceptions to the direct use and quotation of Shakespeare's poems.

Towards the beginning of the book, the Earl of Southampton tells Shakespeare of the marriage contract which his guardian Lord Burghley persuaded him to sign while a child, promising to marry Burghley's granddaughter, Elizabeth de Vere. Shakespeare is incensed at the way the poem *Narcissus* – written at Burghley's behest by his secretary John Clapham – has been deliberately constructed to apply pressure to Southampton to marry. The 'sonnet' which Shakespeare then writes in partial response is my own invention:

Lord of laughter, you showed me Narcissus,
A poem whose heart is hollowed by power;
Falsely addressed, it pretends to kiss us,

Telling of beauty, Cupid's sweet bower;
Yet cold hearts form cold minds, eyes lose their sight;
Stealing our childhood, it counsels good faith.
Framed by deceit, the sun's fatal glower
Reversing all virtue, makes permanent night.
In Hell's own smithies, Authority labours,
Shadow on shadow, reversing the year;
And what is more wretched, than making wretched,
When, lacking all mercy, he sheds no tear?
    Then punish him not for what he may say;
    A mind without light can never see day.

Southampton tears up the sonnet on the grounds that it is likely to endanger Shakespeare's life if it should ever fall into Lord Burghley's hands. By so doing, I hope I made it reasonably plain to the reader that the poem is not one of Shakespeare's own surviving sonnets.

The second and only other use of an imitation sonnet occurs during the narrative sequence when Shakespeare encounters and is rejected by Emilia Bassano. He then finds an answering love in Lucia Florio.

My purpose in suggesting this change of loves was to parallel the more recent scholarly view that John Florio's wife appears a more likely candidate for the role of dark lady than the traditional candidate of Emilia Bassano. During this narrative sequence Shakespeare makes a pass at Emilia, who says she is faithful to Lord Hunsdon. When Shakespeare persists with his suit, she bites his hand to emphasise her point. Later, when Shakespeare meets his former (and future) patron Lord Hunsdon, the wily old nobleman enquires how Shakespeare received the wound to his hand. Shakespeare replies that he was bitten 'by a faithful female hound'. Both men know they are talking about Emilia.

Since (perhaps unsurprisingly) there appeared to be no sonnet entirely appropriate to the circumstances of that change of loves, I constructed an imitation sonnet which was aimed to express Shakespeare's regret at his unrequited love for Emilia Bassano. It seemed to me that I should attempt do my best to include at least an oblique reference to a hound or faithful hound.

If I hear music in the painted day,
Drawing myself towards those fateful sounds,
And all my thoughts move outward to the lay,
Like lines of scent on which run faithful hounds,
Then I must hide my thoughts in careful praise
Which, praising you, fall short of what I feel.
If I should moan your loss, make better days
The sad account of my most bitter meal,
Your fingers on the cloth, touching their hem,
Press me to sit and watch your subtle hands;
The singular white thoughts which rise from them,
Graceful as hinds towards that hidden land.
   O, let me sit beside you while you play,
   Allowing thoughts to alter night for day.

As with the first imitation sonnet, I tried to signal to the reader that the poem did not survive (in this case Shakespeare burns it immediately after writing it) and that therefore it was my own construction.

The only other verses I have attempted are a few pieces of doggerel which Southampton writes in order to give passing voice to Marlowe's death. Since they are obviously not from Shakespeare himself and do not raise any questions of authorship, I shall not reproduce them here or discuss them further.

Finally, I am strongly aware that the fact that I have used Shakespeare's sonnets for the purposes of my own narrative necessarily affects the way in which such sonnets are read. For those readers who are interested to look at certain individual sonnets again, outside the impulsion of the novel's own narrative, and in the order in which Shakespeare himself arranged them, I have drawn up a list of the pages on which each occurs and, alongside them in darker letters, the number of that sonnet in Shakespeare's 154-sonnet sequence. (For the purposes of this book, I used an Oxford University Press edition of the sonnets, but many other editions are available, too.)